Terror in Tombstone

Former lawman Rance Toller and his lover Angie Sutter foil a stagecoach robbery just outside the frontier settlement of Tombstone, Arizona, and in the process capture the notorious gunfighter Johnny Ringo.

As a result, Rance is persuaded to accept the vacant position of town marshal, formerly held by one of the famous Earp brothers. Unfortunately, he soon falls foul of the Big Silver mining operators led by E.B. Gage, who want the law on their terms.

With the dubious help of his new friend, Doc Holliday, Rance has to fight for his life against Gage's ruthless enforcers, as well as take on a band of murderous cattle rustlers and the vengeful Ringo, who has escaped a jail cell with mysterious ease. It is not long before brutal bloody violence explodes on the streets of Tombstone.

By the same author

Blood on the Land
The Devil's Work
The Iron Horse
Pistolero
The Lawmen
The Outlaw Trail

Terror in Tombstone

Paul Bedford

A Black Horse Western
ROBERT HALE

© Paul Bedford 2016
First published in Great Britain 2016

ISBN 978-0-7198-1937-7

The Crowood Press
The Stable Block
Crowood Lane
Ramsbury
Marlborough
Wiltshire SN8 2HR

www.crowood.com

Robert Hale is an imprint
of The Crowood Press

Typeset by Catherine Williams, Knebworth

Printed and bound in Great Britain by
CPI Group (UK) Ltd, Croydon CR0 4YY

CHAPTER ONE

The heavy crash reverberated around the low barren hills and resulted in both riders reining in sharply.

'Apaches?' queried the female breathlessly. There could be no disguising the raw fear that distorted her normally attractive features.

'I very much doubt it,' responded her male companion with far greater composure. 'Indians don't carry sawn-off shotguns. They're useless for hunting.' He paused momentarily, before adding hopefully, 'You stay here while I check it out.'

Angie Sutter emphatically shook her head. 'Like hell I will! You might need someone to watch your back and I don't see anyone else around here taking that job on.'

Rance Toller stared at her fiercely for a moment, before emitting a deep sigh and allowing his expression to soften. 'Just once it would be nice if you did as you were told.'

Without waiting for a response, he slid out of the saddle and led his horse towards the source of the detonation. He carried a sawn-off shotgun of his own, which in itself was a strange weapon for a simple traveller to be carrying. Most contented themselves with a belt gun and maybe a rifle.

From beyond a sharp rise there came a very feminine high-pitched scream. Handing the reins to Angie, Rance instructed, 'Tether the animals below the crest and follow on with your Winchester. Stay back of me and *don't* try any heroics!' This time there was a cold edge to his voice that suggested he just wouldn't tolerate any further dispute.

As he moved off up the rise, Angie levered in a cartridge from the tubular magazine. It occurred to her that they really should have avoided whatever trouble lay in store, but then one of Rance's qualities that so attracted her was that he just wouldn't back down ... ever!

The dust-coated stagecoach had ground to an enforced halt at the bottom of a draw. The legend, Arizona Mail and Stage Company, was painted on the door in fading gold. Unseen by all those involved, Rance took in the whole situation in one practised glance. The driver, unhurt, sat with his gloved hands held high. The guard, wounded, was sprawled on his side on the hard bench seat, groaning in pain. On the ground lay a dull green Wells Fargo strongbox. It was still locked, but unlikely to remain that way.

The passengers, five in total, were lined up alongside the stagecoach. All appeared to be unhurt, but the only woman amongst them was building up a good head of steam.

'You touch me again and I'll make more noise than you can stand,' she shrieked with a pretty fair impression of hysteria.

The heavily muffled character standing before her guffawed. 'There's not another mortal soul around for miles, so scream all you want, lady. Only, just hand over those baubles while you're at it.'

Abruptly recognizing that her theatrics were wasted, the woman very reluctantly did as instructed. 'I hope you die real slow, mister,' she spat out venomously. 'It's supposed to be *me* taking *your* money. That's why I came out to this hellhole.' Hardened beyond her years, her occupation was suddenly very apparent to all those present who hadn't already guessed it.

There were two other 'road agents' in the gang and one of them was getting impatient. 'It'll be old age kills us if we don't get moving!' So saying, he stepped up to the strongbox and aimed the butt of his shotgun at the brass padlock. That attention grabbing action marked the point of no return for Rance Toller. Still unnoticed, he could have quite easily just backed off and let the robbery proceed. Problem was, that just wasn't in his nature.

Drawing back the hammers of his sawn-off, he called out, 'There's a scatter-gun aimed right at your back, mister. Either you or your compadres moves a muscle an' you get to dying!'

The outlaw's heavy gun froze in mid swing. The third man, stationed by the team of horses, snatched a surprised glance over at the newcomer. 'He ain't joshing, Johnny. He's got you lined up good.'

The owner of that given name eased his head to the right and fixed his companion with a piercing stare. A bandana obscured most of his face, but didn't affect the clarity of his speech. 'You mention any more of my moniker and you won't see another sunset, you moron!'

As that man twitched and lowered his head, Johnny called back over his shoulder, 'I don't know where you sprang from, stranger, but you'd best hightail it if you know what's good for you.' With that, he kept his arms rigid, but very slowly began to pivot on his feet.

Rance could have ended it there and then by shooting the man dead, except that cold-blooded killings went against the grain. But then the outlaw over by the passengers found his voice again. 'You got two loads in that big gun, stranger, and there's *three* of us. *And* we're spread out. *And* you make a mighty fine target yourself. So what you gonna do, huh? *Huh?*' As he spoke, his hand began to inch towards the revolver in his belt. He clearly had little regard for the safety of his accomplice.

From behind Rance there came the comforting crash of a Winchester discharging. The bullet kicked up dust right at the feet of the gloating desperado. Jerking instinctively backwards, he flung his hands above his head. His question had been comprehensively answered and suddenly he wasn't so cocky any more.

'Reckon I'm doing all I need to do,' remarked Rance coolly.

Amazingly, the man called Johnny was completely unfazed by the unexpected gunshot and continued with his turn until he directly faced their mysterious assailants. His eyebrows lifted in mild surprise when he realized that one of them was a woman and an attractive one at that. 'Well, well, well. And there was I thinking we were up against *dos hombres*!'

Rance had heard more than enough. 'All of you drop your weapons. Now!'

'And if we don't, what will you do?' responded Johnny softly. 'Kill us all?' Even though his features weren't visible, he clearly possessed an icy calm that would have unnerved a lesser opponent. His eyes were like chips of ice as he continued. 'Only you see, I was born to die anyway. It's amazing that I've lasted so long really. Maybe it's because I can read people. If you were going to gun me down like a dog, you'd have done it by now.'

For the first time, Rance's eyes locked onto those of the other man. The challenge was unmistakeable and it brought back memories of similar occasions many years before in the dusty cow towns of the mid West. His features tightened without him even realizing it and Rance abruptly found that he was talking through gritted teeth.

'There's more than one way to skin a cat, mister,' he remarked, every word coated with menace. With that he slowly advanced on his uncooperative prisoner, at the same time deftly swapping the shotgun over to his left hand and drawing the Remington revolver from its holster.

The man called Johnny took in the neat manoeuvre, specifically noting the make of handgun. With its strong frame, a Remington was often times the weapon of choice for lawmen and at that moment he began to feel an unaccustomed flicker of unease. The strongly built stranger advanced on him remorselessly until they were only feet apart. There was about him an intense aura of latent violence. With his own weapon still held above his head, the outlaw began to experience the feeling of uncomfortable vulnerability.

Rance maintained eye contact for a few seconds more and then, with the speed of a striking snake, slammed the barrel of his revolver up against the side of Johnny's head. No amount of arrogance could absorb such a clout and the 'road agent' rocked under the force of it and dropped to his knees.

'Hit him again, mister!' cried out the female passenger enthusiastically. She turned to the others and added, 'Did you see that? He buffaloed that son of a bitch real good.'

Her fellow passengers remained silent, apparently mesmerized by the turn of events.

Rance's hard eyes flicked over to her, but before he could make any comment there was a tremendous detonation directly before him. Whether by accident or design, both barrels of Johnny's shotgun discharged harmlessly into the air. Instinctively, Rance kicked out at the heavy weapon and it tumbled from the outlaw's weakened grip. Still stunned from the violent blow, he appeared to be wholly unaware of what he'd actually done. Yet the sudden distraction of noise and smoke was all that his two accomplices needed. Turning tail, they raced off to where they had tethered their horses and a few moments later there came the pounding of hoofs.

Rance holstered his revolver and glanced down at his swaying captive. 'Looks like I'm going to have to make do with just you, so let's get a better look.' So saying, he yanked at the bandana over Johnny's face. Lean features and a well-maintained moustache came into view; along with a bloodied left cheek where the gun barrel had struck him. The eyes glittered with vicious hatred ... and possibly something else as well. In his time, Rance had encountered many bad men. He himself had been considered such on occasion, but this fellow's stare was tinged with madness. Bending down, he snatched a well-worn Colt Army from Johnny's belt holster and tucked it into his own waistband.

'The best place for you is a jail cell,' he wholeheartedly remarked. 'And a strong one at that.' Even as he spoke, Rance was aware of Angie coming up behind him. 'Thanks for your help,' he added softly.

The young woman chuckled. 'Think nothing of it … but I can't imagine what you used to do without me.'

Before he could respond, there was movement around the stagecoach. The passengers couldn't quite believe the remarkable turn of events and were milling about, congratulating themselves. They even managed to call thanks over to their two rescuers, but kept well clear of the glowering 'road agent'. The driver had more practical matters on his mind.

'I don't know who you folks are, but the thank yous will have to wait. Philpot's hurt bad. We need to get him inside the coach and on to the sawbones in Tombstone. The doc there ain't much, but he's all we've got.'

'That's where we were headed,' replied Rance. 'Is there any kind of law there?'

'Not anything like as much as there used to be,' the grizzled driver cryptically responded. 'Certainly no one in the town limits. Behan's still the County Sheriff, but we've got mail on board so that'd make this hold-up a federal matter as well. If anyone's done appointed another U. S. Marshal, that is.'

The man's comments clearly required a great deal of clarification, but there was no time for that.

'Just so long as we can get this cuss behind bars,' Rance stated, brusquely pulling Johnny to his feet. 'We'll tie his hands to the luggage rack and he can ride up top with the rest of the baggage.'

The driver, about to enlist the passengers to help with his wounded companion, peered at Rance enquiringly. 'You really don't know who this pus weasel is, do you?'

Rance shrugged his shoulders. 'We're both strangers in these parts.'

The other man shook his head wonderingly. 'This here only happens to be Johnny Ringo. The most feared pistolero in the whole southwest!'

At the mention of his name, that individual produced a cold smile that completely failed to reach his eyes. 'And you two pilgrims are going to regret ever having crossed me. If the Earps couldn't stop me, what chance do you have?'

Rance's bewilderment was completely genuine. 'The who?'

CHAPTER TWO

The town of Tombstone had shaky foundations, both figuratively and literally, which were based purely on greed. It was a mining town and as such existed only for as long as the local mines continued to produce silver in vast quantities. The diggings infested the land surrounding the settlement and many of them even stretched under the hastily erected buildings, periodically bringing them tumbling down. Hoists and smelters were manned non-stop, as men worked like ants to extract as much profit from the land as possible. With stamp mills pulverising ore bearing rock and saw mills providing much needed timber supports, the cacophony of sound around the settlement was ever-present. The precious metal was responsible for putting the city on the map and likely to make it the county seat of the newly formed Cochise County, but it was also to blame for attracting a lot of hard and dangerous men. And one of those was John Peters Ringo.

The seething discontent that always pervaded his troubled mind reached fever pitch that afternoon in November 1881. Having *almost* robbed the stagecoach on its journey from Tucson to Tombstone, he now found himself trussed up on

13

top of it like a Thanksgiving turkey. As blood trickled down his gashed cheek, Ringo vowed lethal retribution on the complete stranger who had apprehended him. He had killed better men for much less provocation. And then there was the attractive little bitch that accompanied him. John Ringo had no idea what her angle was, except that her sex wouldn't save her when the time came. But all that would have to wait, because as the stagecoach rattled its way along Fremont Street, named after the territorial governor and famous explorer, John C. Fremont, he knew that he must surely be destined for a jail cell … at least for a short while. And the prospect of even temporary incarceration only served to feed the barely contained rage that was building up inside. As blood trickled into his mouth, he glowered over at the two newcomers as they followed the stage into town.

Rance and Angie kept well clear of the dust cloud trailing the primitive conveyance and gazed about at their new home with genuine interest. Even the relentless hammering sounds failed to distract them. The buildings were constructed from either wood or adobe and bordered spacious streets laid out in a uniform grid pattern. Everywhere they looked, there was the bustling activity of a thriving boomtown. What appealed even more, was that although it was late autumn, the weather was warm and dry; a stark contrast to what they would have experienced had they remained in Dakota Territory. Neither of them knew what they were actually going to do to earn a living in Tombstone, but they were about to make a good first impression on the citizenry.

As the stagecoach came to a halt in front of the Wells Fargo office, the driver bellowed out, 'We've been attacked. Bud Philpot's been shot. Someone fetch the doc, pronto!'

A sizeable crowd soon gathered, attracted by the unusual sight of Johnny Ringo immobilized and helpless. It was then that the driver made the announcement that would have such an effect on Rance and Angie's future in the mining town. 'These folks faced down the road agents and saved the strongbox.'

There was an increase in chatter amongst the sightseers, then a self-important voice piped up in the rear, urging people to, 'Make way there, make way,' and the driver scowled.

'Here comes that asshole, Behan!'

Hostility to authority was nothing new for Rance. 'County sheriff, huh?'

The other man grunted. 'More like tax collector. He gets ten per cent of all the take and in a place like this that's a lot of dinero.'

The tin star finally appeared. Attached to it was a dapper gent, slim, medium height and extremely well-dressed for a frontier town. He gazed at Rance and Angie with genuine curiosity, but then his eyes lurched up to their prisoner and his jaw dropped. Struggling to get through the gawkers, he had not noticed the reluctant passenger.

'What the hell are you doing up there?' he finally managed.

Ringo sneered. 'These poor fools think I was trying to rob them. Truth is, I just thought that strongbox would be safer with me, is all.'

At that moment another individual forced his way through the spectators. He was a good-looking fellow in his thirties who possessed store bought clothes and a business-like manner. The driver thawed immediately and offered a smile of recognition.

'How do, Mr Williams. Ignore anything that bull turd up top says. His gang shot Bud and would have cleaned us out if it hadn't been for these folks. And I don't even know their names.'

The newcomer's keen eyes scanned Rance and Angie. His gaze lingered hungrily on the young woman for a long moment, before he politely tipped his hat and then extended his right hand to her companion. As Rance took it, he announced, 'Well, mine is Drew Williams. I'm the Wells Fargo agent in these parts. If that strongbox *had* been cleaned out, we would have had to stand a big loss. So it seems my employers owe you a debt of gratitude, Mr...?'

'Toller,' that man replied for the first time since arriving in the Territory of Arizona. 'Rance Toller. And this is my travelling companion, Angie Sutter.'

Williams's attention temporarily left them as he glanced over at Sheriff Johnny Behan. 'This is a county matter, so you've got jurisdiction. I need that man locked up and cooling his heels, Johnny,' he briskly demanded. 'I'll be pressing charges for murderous assault and attempted robbery. I want him up before Judge Spicer tomorrow morning, you hear?'

The lawman nodded reluctantly, before clambering up onto the stagecoach to release his new prisoner. That man made no attempt at resistance, but as he was being led away, he suddenly tugged free and turned to face Rance. 'I'll be seeing you around, mister.' His voice was low and dangerous, matching his malevolent stare. 'You made a big mistake tangling with the Cowboys.'

As Ringo finally allowed himself to be marched off,

Williams attempted to make light of the obvious threat. 'Don't pay him no mind, Rance. His kind are all talk … usually.'

Rance regarded him steadily. 'Oh, I know all about his kind, Mr Williams. There's always at least one in every town. Just who are these *Cowboys* anyway?'

The Wells Fargo agent at least had the good grace to appear uncomfortable. 'They're a band of rustlers and low lifes who got run out of Texas by the Rangers. Arizona's about the only place left for people like them now. They call themselves Cowboys because *other people's* cows are their business and they've taken to wearing those red sashes to stand out from everyone else. If you ask me, they just look plain foolish. Anyway, they steal cattle down in Mexico and sell the animals north of the border. There's a big market for beef in Tombstone, what with the diggings an' all and of course the army always needs meat as well.'

'I know,' Rance replied. 'Angie and I came down from Wyoming with a big herd. Sold them at Fort Grant for top dollar. Just a shame we were only in for a percentage.'

Williams was curious. 'You two made any plans as to how to pass the time or are you just in Tombstone for the climate?'

Rance laughed and then regarded Angie warmly before answering. 'I thought I might try my hand at prospecting. After all, they say there's no fool like an old fool. First, though, we're going to find a hotel and rest up for a while. We've been on the trail for an awful long time.'

Williams regarded him keenly. 'The best claims have already been taken by the big operators and somehow I don't see you grubbing in the earth.' He shrugged his shoulders.

'But no matter. If you're agreeable, I'll take you over to the Grand Hotel on Allen Street. It's the best in town and the least Wells Fargo can do is stand you the first couple of nights there.'

Angie's tired features lit up with almost childish glee at the prospect of both a roof and mattress. 'And I'll bet they've got a bath house there, haven't they? Or at least a tub. My, my, I can almost *feel* that hot water.'

Both men laughed. The shipping agent's proposal had obviously been accepted, but it was to be some time before they actually got there. The doctor, reeking of cheap liquor, had finally arrived to tend to the wounded guard and demanded assurances of payment for his dubious services. With that settled, Williams then led his guests to the Dexter Feed and Livery Stables. Only when their animals' welfare had been attended to courtesy of Wells Fargo, did they at last reach the hotel. It was a substantial two storey wooden building, complete with a veranda on the upper floor, all of which hinted at a level of luxury that neither visitor had ever experienced.

The sudden flurry of gunshots took them all by surprise, but it was Rance who reacted first. His long guns were wrapped up in his bedroll, so he simply let them fall to the ground. Then, with practised speed, he drew and cocked his Remington, at the same time swinging around to face the source of the detonations.

From just across the way, two men burst out of the Occidental Saloon; a name that hinted at an unusually educated owner. They were firing indiscriminately at each other, hot lead flying in all directions until finally one of them stopped a bullet. That man dropped to his knees in the dust, blood gushing from a fatal wound in his throat. His killer, grubby and unkempt, looked on in whiskey-soaked detachment until his victim finally choked to death on his own fluids. Only then did he holster his revolver. Oblivious to the startled onlookers, he was about to drift back into the saloon when he glanced idly around him and twitched with surprise as he noticed Rance facing him with a drawn weapon. The two men eyed each other for a few moments before the miner shrugged disinterestedly and turned away.

Watching the casual assassin depart, Rance slowly lowered the hammer on his weapon and turned to Drew Williams. 'This town's run kind of reckless, ain't it? Where's all the law? Why's everyone packing firearms?'

The Wells Fargo agent grunted with surprise and ran a trembling hand over his face. 'You really don't know anything about what's gone on down here, do you? Well, I'll tell you. There *used* to be plenty of law around here and most of it was the Earps. Virgil was both town marshal and a deputy U. S. Marshal. His brothers Wyatt and Morgan were special deputies and they had some gun thug named Doc Holliday backing their play as well. They ran a tight ship. No carrying firearms within the city limits and no rowdy behaviour. It was only a matter of time before they and the Cowboys came to blows. And when it happened it was something to behold. A real bloodbath. Three Cowboys died, shot to pieces. Virgil was crippled and Morgan wounded. Wyatt didn't even get a scratch. The Cowboys vowed revenge and killed Morgan some weeks later. Wyatt and Doc went gun crazy and joined up with Texas Jack Vermillion, Turkey Creek Johnson and some others. They hunted Curly Bill Brocius and three more assassins down outside of town, before fleeing to Colorado.

Unfortunately that left Johnny Ringo and the rest of the Cowboys to carry on as before, only now there's no law in Tombstone and nobody seems to want the job. And I haven't talked so much since I laid my pa to rest!'

Rance shook his head. 'Seems a shame. Thriving town like this. What about that Behan fellow?'

Williams laughed scornfully. 'Behan ain't worth a damn. He glad-hands anybody and everybody and all the time takes his cut of the taxes. But enough of all this. Let's get you folks situated inside.'

As the three of them entered the Grand Hotel, Angie scrutinized Rance anxiously. A blind man on a galloping horse couldn't have missed the interest on his features as Williams described the state of affairs in town. The chilling thought that 'once a lawman, always a lawman', came to mind and left her feeling sick to her stomach.

It was late the next morning when Mayor John Clum knocked gently on their bedroom door. As befitted his full-time profession, he had stood and listened for a few moments first. Murmured conversation and a distinctly feminine giggle told him nothing except that Rance Toller was not alone. Total silence followed his polite tap and then the door eased open, revealing an apparently empty room. Disconcerted, the visitor tentatively advanced across the threshold and literally jumped with shock.

Off to his right, laying full length along the wall, was a man with a gun. The cocked revolver was pointing directly at his torso and for a brief heart-stopping moment, he actually thought that he was about to die. Then the hammer eased down and a young woman rose up from behind the double bed. Clum stared from one to the other before grabbing a handkerchief from the breast pocket of his jacket. Moping his brow, he exclaimed, 'Christ, mister! You scared the bejesus out of me and I'm not even Irish.'

Rance got to his feet and regarded him without any show of remorse. 'We weren't expecting visitors and old habits die hard.'

Clum favoured him with a wary smile. 'Well, actually, that's what I want to talk to you about. I've got a proposition for you.'

Angie moved swiftly around the bed towards him. She swept her fine sandy hair back from her face with both hands and then settled her eyes on his. The hostility in them was unmistakeable.

'The only thing you know about Rance is that he stopped a stage being robbed,' she snapped heatedly. 'Which means you're most likely looking for him to put on a tin star again. Thing is, he doesn't do that sort of work anymore, so leave us alone.'

She shut her attractive mouth like a trap, annoyed at her inadvertent slip. Clum smiled shrewdly. He would have quite happily conversed with the shapely young woman all day long, but sadly had other business to transact. Spreading his hands out in a gesture of supplication, he implored, 'Just hear me out, Mr Toller. That's all I ask. If you're not interested in what I have to say, I won't trouble you again.' A professional grin lit up his face. 'Fair enough?'

Rance glanced fondly at his feisty companion. God, she's gorgeous when she's angry, he thought and not for the first time. Waving their visitor to a chair, he replied, 'I guess it can't hurt to listen.'

21

That man got straight to the point. 'I have a considerable personal stake in Tombstone. I'm the mayor, the postmaster and I own and operate the *Epitaph* newspaper. Since the Earps left, we've had no town marshal and no federal law. For what he's worth, Behan handles the county, but he's got no jurisdiction here in town. The Committee for Public Safety passed an ordinance that no firearms should be carried within the town limits, but there's nobody to enforce it and so most of the wilder elements just ignore it.'

Rance now fully comprehended the situation, because in truth he had seen it all before. 'Some of those *wilder elements* wouldn't just happen to be from Texas, would they?'

The mayor nodded glumly, but before he had chance to comment, Rance had more to say. 'And you *good* people are all worried about the effect an increase in violence is going to have on your businesses. Am I right?'

Clum hadn't missed the gentle sarcasm, but chose to ignore it. 'I've come here with the authority to make you chief of police, if you'll take the job. This town is in trouble and I ... *we've* no one else to turn to. If you accept, we'll pay you $200 a month and you can keep this room free of charge until further notice. What do you say to that?'

Rance chuckled briefly and then his expression became deadly serious. He walked in silence over to the window and peered down on Allen Street for a long moment. There were plenty of men on the thoroughfare and a goodly number were carrying weapons ... unlawfully. Somehow, such behaviour offended his sense of the natural order of things. Then he looked over at his lovely companion. He noted the imploring look in her eyes and fleetingly his new resolve weakened. Reluctantly breaking the contact, he turned to face the mayor and his jaw tightened.

'You'll pay me $250 a month *and* $1 for each arrest. And, since there don't appear to be anyone else in your police department, I'll take the title of Marshal. It sits better with me and also everyone will know that I alone carry the law in this town. Agreed?'

Clum blinked owlishly at him for a moment and then nodded slowly. 'I should be able to sell it to the city fathers.'

Rance suddenly had other matters on his mind. He could feel Angie's eyes boring into him like gimlets. 'Oh I'm sure you can. Now if you'll excuse us, it looks like I've got some explaining to do.'

Mayor Clum smiled his understanding, but he still had one more thing to impart. 'It's probably a good thing you're a lawman now. Leastways for as long as you're staying in Tombstone.'

Rance stared at him uncomprehendingly.

'Only the thing is, Johnny Ringo escaped from jail last night. So now, if he comes after you, at least you'll be legally entitled to wear a gun!'

CHAPTER THREE

Marshal Toller stared out at the sea of activity in the street beyond his new office. The hurly-burly was a fair reflection of his mind, which just happened to be a seething morass of conflicting thoughts. He knew that he had better damn well get them under control before he stepped outside wearing *the badge.* That resembled a medieval shield with a five-pointed star at its centre and its presence on his chest had changed everything. For a start it could get him killed very quickly.

Not so long ago that fact would not have bothered anyone else, but now he had Angie to share his life with and along with her blissful presence came a definite hankering to survive. Although some fifteen years his junior, she considered herself to be his equal and never held back from telling him exactly what she thought. Having lost her husband to a murderous assassin in Dakota Territory, she too had every desire that Rance should reach old age. The problem was that taking on the marshal's job in a frontier boomtown had created some very long odds on that happening and he could still hear her angry words ringing in his ears.

A shot rang out somewhere in town and was soon followed by others. The jarring sounds brought him sharply out of his reverie and a deeply tanned forehead creased in a heavy frown. His normally orderly mind profoundly resented the lawlessness that pervaded the town. After years spent upholding the law, it was almost like a personal insult.

'God damn it,' he exclaimed to the empty room. 'This stops now!'

After checking the loads in his shotgun, he strode briskly to the door and lifted the latch. There he paused to draw in two deep breaths. From that point on, his movements would have to be measured and deliberate. Stepping outside, the lawman moved one pace to his right so that he had the timber wall of the jailhouse to his back. Holding the deadly sawn-off in both hands, he carefully scrutinized the length of Fremont Street. Another gunshot crashed out, louder this time, followed by a deal of raucous laughter. The noise enabled him to pinpoint the source as being on Allen Street and dime to a dollar, the trouble would be in the Occidental Saloon.

Earlier in the day he had walked all of Tombstone's main thoroughfares as a private citizen and he had soon discovered that the majority of the saloons and hotels mingled together on Allen Street and of all of them, the Occidental seemed to be the rowdiest. The term *snake pit* came to mind, so that was definitely the place to start. To get there, he needed to take a right onto 4th Street, followed by a left onto Allen.

As in so many towns before, the new marshal's progress was unhurried and essentially defensive. He took the direct route across the street; so minimizing his time in the open and then kept close to the buildings as he moved towards the junction. He was aware of one or two residents regarding him curiously, but since none seemed to pose a potential threat he ignored them. As he turned the corner, two more shots rang out. From the erratic frequency of them, Rance realized that bloodletting was unlikely. It was 'joy' firing and someone was having quite a shindig!

4th Street was completely empty, so he briefly increased speed. The locals had obviously either fled or allowed their curiosity to get the better of them. Reaching the junction with Allen Street, he snuggled up to the side of Hafford's Saloon and peered around the corner. Three doors down, a crowd of gawkers were gathered around the entrance to the Occidental. He licked his lips and took a steadying breath. This was to be his first big test as Tombstone's new marshal.

Moving out from cover, Rance cautiously passed the entrances to Hafford's and then the Cosmopolitan Hotel and fetched up behind the onlookers.

'Step aside!' he demanded in a tone that was harsh and uncompromising. It served to catch their attention and most of them turned to view the new arrival. What they saw was a strongly built individual of above average height, wearing a black, flat crowned hat and clearly displaying a badge of office. That and the vicious looking scatter-gun were more than enough to clear a wide avenue to the saloon's swing doors. From there he carefully scrutinized the interior.

Down the entire right hand side of the large room, there ran a solidly built bar, behind which hung a huge and quite magnificent gilt mirror. Beautifully polished, the glass reflected the light from the numerous kerosene lamps dotted around. It was clearly the centrepiece of the establishment and had to have been freighted, no doubt at massive expense, all the way from San Francisco or the like. A group of men were drunkenly cavorting in the middle of the saloon, occasionally aiming their revolvers at the exceptionally tempting target. They could be distinguished from the other occupants by the garish red sashes that they wore around their waists. The weapons had obviously been recently triggered, as clouds of powder smoke were still collected in the eaves of the single storey building. Wood chippings from the much-abused ceiling were strewn about the bare floor boarding.

The heavily sweating barman was clearly desperately unhappy with the situation. His right hand nervously disappeared under the counter for a few seconds as though checking on something. Rance grunted knowingly. He obviously wasn't the only one with immediate access to a shotgun. A glance at the rest of the customers satisfied him that they were mostly grubby and unkempt prospectors, rapidly drinking themselves into oblivion. The Occidental clearly didn't appeal to the town's 'high rollers'.

Then a cadaverous individual, sitting alone in the far corner, caught his attention.

The man wore a black frock coat and was nursing a glass of whiskey, obviously poured from the half empty bottle before him. Although quite evidently isolated from the raucous proceedings, he was nevertheless taking a keen interest and Rance marked him down as someone to watch.

The total appraisal had taken bare moments and like it or not, it was time to make a move. He would have been far happier with a deputy covering the room from the back door, but it was not to be. All alone and conscious of his heart beating like an anvil strike, Tombstone's new marshal shouldered his way through the swing doors and into a world of trouble.

*

The best rooms on the first floor of the Grand Hotel just happened to face out onto Allen Street and so it was with almost inevitable bad timing that Angie Sutter saw her lover approach the saloon. The onlookers parted like the Red Sea before Moses and then Rance stood for a while, surveying the interior. She felt a frantic urge to cry out to him, but knew that that would only serve to push him off balance and then, suddenly, it was too late anyway. He had entered the saloon ... unaided. Without back up of any kind.

Overcome by guilt at the harsh words they had earlier exchanged, Angie grabbed her Winchester and raced for the bedroom door. She might not have been able to prevent his becoming a lawman again, but at least she could act as an unofficial deputy.

If Rance Toller had been surrounded by armed assistants, he would have ploughed on into the centre of the room ... but he wasn't. Consequently he moved cautiously through the swing doors and then sidestepped to his left. Standing with his back to solid timber, he regarded the drunken yahoos balefully. They were completely oblivious to his presence and one of them was about to overstep the mark. A tall, greasy haired individual aimed his Colt at the oh so tempting mirror and cocked the hammer.

Enough was enough. Rance cocked both hammers of his shotgun, took aim at the ceiling above the trouble causers and squeezed one trigger. In the enclosed space, the big weapon discharged with a stunning roar that took everyone by surprise. As wood chippings showered over them, the rowdies peered around in astonishment. Finally their eyes settled on the man with the smoking gun.

'You stupid son of a bitch,' snarled one with slick black hair and a livid scar on his left cheek. 'You'll pay for that!'

Rance moved carefully forward and levelled the sawn-off. For the first time, his badge was visible to the room's occupants. 'Actually it's you fellas that's going to pay,' he remarked softly. 'For all and any damage to this establishment.'

Another of the Cowboys, his wits less addled than the rest, demanded, 'Just who the hell are you, mister?'

The lawman favoured him with a bleak smile. 'I'm Rance Toller. I carry the law in Tombstone and you all are breaking it. Every man here that's packing a gun will place it on the bar or face the consequences.'

The same man sneered and glanced at his cronies before replying. 'And what if we don't, law dog? Huh? What then?'

Rance regarded him calmly for a moment and then suddenly advanced towards him until the gaping muzzles of his shotgun were mere inches from the man's stomach. 'I'll open you up so that everyone in this shithole will see what you had for breakfast. Savvy? After that it won't much matter what happens to me, because you'll be dead as a wagon tyre.'

That man examined Rance's weathered features and turned pale. There was something about the new lawman's chill demeanour that suggested it was no idle threat. Even as his companions reached for their six-guns, he cried out, 'Leave them be, God damn it! He means it!'

'Damn right I mean it,' Rance barked. 'Now shuck those belt guns. All of you!'

Very reluctantly the men began to comply ... with the exception of the scarred hombre at the rear, who obviously had little concern for his friends' survival. Shielded by the others, he swiftly drew his Colt Army and swung round his buddies to draw a bead on Rance. That man heard the hammer cocking, but was simply unable to react in time.

The inevitable gunshot crashed out, but it came from a completely unexpected quarter. The cowboy emitted a strangled cry and fell sideways, mortally stricken. As he did so, his trigger finger contracted and the Colt added to the noise and smoke in the saloon. The large calibre bullet slammed into the centre of the splendid mirror and sent shards of glass flying over the bar area. The barkeeper howled out in horror, either because of the bloody gash on his hand or the irrevocable damage to his prized display piece.

With no further resistance and the men disarmed, Rance stepped back so as to view his saviour. The rail thin individual in the far corner got slowly to his feet, a sardonic smile on his face and the smoking revolver still in his hand. 'Seems like you Cowboys just can't keep out of trouble.'

'You had no call to go and do that, Holliday,' protested one of them bitterly.

That man shrugged disinterestedly and sauntered over to join Rance. 'Law and order every time, that's what I say,' Holliday remarked, as his piercing eyes settled on Tombstone's marshal. 'And our latest lawman seemed to be doing pretty good by himself.'

At that moment the swing doors burst open and the business end of a Winchester came into view. Holliday levelled his weapon, but Rance rapidly stepped in front of him. 'Whoa there, friend. Right now, she's the closest thing I've got to a deputy. Be a big shame to pop a cap on her.'

Angie pulled up short when she saw Rance alive and well.

The relief on her face was plain to see and he loved her all the more because of it.

'You'll get yourself killed, barrelling in to a strange building like that,' he gently chided and then favoured her with a beaming smile. As she moved over to join him, he turned to the man in the black frockcoat. 'This gentleman just saved my life. That pus weasel called you Holliday. Would that be the Doc Holliday that supposedly fled to Colorado with his friend Wyatt Earp?'

Holliday offered a wan smile but before he could reply, a vicious hacking cough arrived seemingly from nowhere. His thin shoulders convulsed and for a few moments he was quite unable to speak. Momentarily taken aback, Rance busied himself by herding the remaining cowboys off the premises, but not before he had made them empty their pockets. 'That'll go some ways towards the cost of a new mirror. You'll get your guns back when you leave town, boys and not before. Pass the word around. Tombstone's got law again!'

As the disgruntled ruffians departed, Rance's attention was then taken by the barkeeper. That unhappy individual had surfaced from under the shards of glass and come round from behind the bar. Blood was dripping from the fingers of his left hand and he aimed a particularly ferocious kick at the head of the dead Cowboy.

'I had to wait weeks for that mirror and now look at it,' he exclaimed angrily. 'It's not even got scrap value!'

Doc Holliday had at last got control of his emaciated frame and snorted dismissively. 'Shouldn't have put it up in a shithole like this then, should you?'

The Occidental's owner scowled at him, but apparently

knew better than to respond. Instead he shambled off to summon the undertaker and Holliday finally managed to answer Rance in a distinctly southern drawl.

'Colorado had its charms, but I don't flee from any son of a bitch. The grim reaper's going to claim me soon enough anyway. As for Wyatt, he just chose to make a … *strategic withdrawal.*'

Rance smiled warmly at him, but his words carried a chill. 'Maybe you should have gone to Colorado anyway. They say the climate's better for a man dying of consumption.'

The two men's eyes locked as Holliday chose his next words carefully. 'It took some grit to come into this nest of vipers all on your lonesome. Perhaps death don't hold any fears for you either.'

'I've been a lawman all my life. It's in my blood and it's all that I know. Problem is, my good friend Angie here doesn't always see it that way. Do you?'

The young woman chose to ignore his question and instead approached Holliday with her right hand outstretched. That man swiftly holstered his revolver and matched her gesture. As his thin bony hand connected with hers, she offered him a dazzling smile.

'You saved Rance's life, Mr Holliday, and I truly thank you for it. If you should ever need help, you have only to call on me.'

Her sincerity was so obviously genuine that his ravaged features softened appreciably. 'My friends call me Doc and believe me when I say there aren't many of those.'

'Doc it is then,' replied Angie firmly.

Rance looked at the two of them and nodded. 'I reckon so.'

Then it was back to business. Replacing the spent cartridge in his shotgun, he announced, 'This establishment has kind of lost its appeal. I'm going out there to spread the good word that the rule of law has returned to Tombstone. You're both welcome to tag along.' Then, glancing hopefully at Angie, he added, 'Just keep back of me, yeah?'

And so the three of them cautiously ventured out onto Allen Street. Of the disarmed and newly impoverished Cowboys there was no sign, but plenty of other folks were milling around, drawn by news of the confrontation in the saloon. John Clum, doubtless in the guise of Editor of the *Epitaph* and sporting a dapper bowler hat, was hurrying towards the new marshal. A good story already beckoned, but he could not have known that for once he was definitely about to be in the right place at the right time.

The bullet caught Angie in the left shoulder and spun her around, so that she was again facing the Occidental. As all strength abruptly left her well-formed legs, the young woman dropped to her knees in the dust. Stunned by the hammer blow, the only sound to escape her lips was a muffled grunt.

Snarling out in animal fury, Rance searched desperately amongst the surprised bystanders for the gunman and he didn't have far to look. Down the street a ways, astride a black horse, Johnny Ringo levered up another cartridge into the breach of his rifle.

'Get her on the ground,' the marshal yelled at Holliday, not realizing that that man was already shielding her with his own body. Then, cocking both hammers of the sawn-off, he raced off towards the assassin. With such exertion his accuracy would be poor, but that mattered little with a scatter-gun. Ringo had twisted in his saddle to take a second shot, but as the gaping muzzles of the twelve-gauge drew rapidly closer, self-preservation took precedence. Spurring his mount into action, he pounded off down the thoroughfare past the intersections of 5th and 6th Street and on out of town. Not one man fired at him, even though there were still plenty of them illegally carrying firearms.

Driven by anger and frustration more than anything, Rance came to a shuddering halt and discharged one barrel at the fleeing figure, but the range was just too great.

'God damn it to hell,' he exclaimed, as the pieces of shot dropped harmlessly to the ground. 'That cockchafer's going to suffer for this!'

Twisting around, he then pounded back to where Angie lay in the dirt with the southerner at her side. Unaware of her condition and fearing for the worst, Rance's face was etched with terrible anxiety. He found her moaning incoherently. A horrifying amount of blood coated her cotton shirt and she was breathing raggedly, as though in shock. Holliday was pressing a handkerchief hard against the entry wound. Rance had seen many people shot, but this was frighteningly different. For once he actually cared very deeply about the victim and it was more than mere exertion that caused his heart to beat like an anvil strike.

'We need to get her inside and find a sawbones,' he gasped.

'He ain't fit to pour pee from a boot,' Holliday responded harshly. 'I'll tend to her myself.'

Rance gazed at him in amazement. 'You?'

The other man glanced up at him sharply. 'Why do you think folks call me Doc? I might be a sporting man now, but back in Georgia I trained as a dentist. I was proud to be a dentist. And extracting teeth's just like extracting bullets … pretty much.'

The lawman regarded him doubtfully. 'Yeah, but will she live?' he queried desperately. Not really wanting to hear the response to that, he ostentatiously reloaded his shotgun and then bellowed down the thoroughfare. 'This is your first and only warning. I'm going inside for a spell. When I come back out on the street, I'll kill any man I see wearing a gun.'

With that, he turned back to his stricken lover and together the two men gently picked her up and carried her towards the hotel. As they reached the threshold, Doc remarked dryly, 'Seeing you work *almost* makes me wish I was a lawman.'

CHAPTER FOUR

Room six in the Grand Hotel was uncomfortably crowded, but Rance Toller barely noticed. He had eyes only for Angie. Her complexion was unhealthily pale and her breathing fitful. Mercifully, she had passed out whilst being carried indoors. The misshapen lead bullet had been painlessly removed and her wound cleaned and bandaged. She was young and strong, but it was far too soon to say whether she would survive.

Even so, Doc Holliday had 'done good' and he was actually feeling rather proud of himself. It was not often that he had been able to say that in recent times. Far too frequently of late, he seemed to end up drinking himself into a stupor or getting into murderous arguments with fellow poker players. He knew exactly why he did it. He was dying of the consumption and no power in the land could change that. Such grim realization had created within him a permanent sense of grievance at the 'dead man's hand' that nature had dealt him. And yet, out of the blue, he seemed to have made two new friends.

As though somehow sensing Holliday's thoughts, Rance tore his gaze away from the woman he loved more than anything and gently placed a hand on his scrawny shoulders. 'You've saved my life and hopefully Angie's as well. I owe you more than I can ever repay.'

The other man smiled self-consciously. 'Your friendship'll do for now,' he replied. 'I've never had too many of them.'

Mayor John Clum regarded the notorious killer dubiously and chose to direct his remarks solely at his new marshal. 'Too often the rule of law is flouted in this town,' he began rather pompously. 'I want you to get out there and find this John Ringo. Bring him to justice. Do whatever it takes and my newspaper will back you all the way.'

Drew Williams was also present and he had his own ideas. 'If I was you I'd pay Johnny Behan a visit. Doesn't it seem mighty strange to you that Ringo got clear of his jail so fast? He couldn't have done it quicker if the locks had been made of hammered shit.'

Rance completely ignored the colourful analogy and merely nodded grimly. Oh yes, he was puzzled all right. 'Why would a county sheriff be in cahoots with one of the rustlers anyway? It makes no sense.'

The Wells Fargo agent snorted. 'It does if you know that the Cowboys help Behan collect his taxes for a percentage. He's no gunhand. He'd struggle to manage without them and believe me, there's a lot of dinero at stake.'

So Rance's course of action was now all too clear. 'Looks like I'll have to start with him then.'

Holliday noisily cleared his throat. 'You mean, we will! It's time that bull turd was brought to account and I want to be there to see it.'

Rance smiled his gratitude, but then suddenly hesitated. 'But what about Angie? I can't leave her here all alone.'

Williams was quick to respond. 'I'll watch over her,' he eagerly suggested. 'My employers want Ringo caught *nearly* as much as you, but I don't have the stomach for gun play. Besides, there's nothing more you can do for her right now, so go and enforce the law.'

Rance slowly nodded agreement, but he wasn't quite finished. His eyes found those of the mayor. 'Just so's this is all done legal, I want *Mr* Holliday sworn in as a deputy, on wages. I have it on good authority that he is a highly respected dentist. As a professional man, he should make a fine lawman.'

John Clum's eyes widened incredulously and he struggled to find any words. In the end he had to settle for a mute nod of assent.

Holliday regarded him calculatingly and simply couldn't resist a slight dig. 'Just how are your teeth anyway, Mr Mayor?'

So it was all settled. Rance kissed the totally oblivious woman lovingly on her forehead and then he and his new deputy left the room. As they did so, he remarked to him, 'Looks like you've *almost* got your wish.'

As the two lawmen made their way towards the county sheriff's office, cautiously and with weapons drawn, Rance had a question. 'If Ringo's such a good shot, how did he miss me and hit Angie?'

'By all accounts he's deadly with a sidearm, but as you doubtless know rifle shooting's different altogether,' offered Holliday reflectively. 'Then again, maybe he hit exactly what he was aiming at. Killing a lawman's a sure way to trouble, but he still had a score to settle. Or he may not have heard that you were badged up and just did it out of spite. What the hell.' He shrugged. 'Who knows with a kill-crazy like him.'

Rance's already grim expression hardened further. His eyes held a burning intensity that boded ill for anyone who got in his way. Holliday recognized the signs and nodded to himself.

'How long you been a lawman anyway?' he queried.

'Too long,' came the terse response, effectively ending any further conversation.

The Sheriff of Cochise County worked out of rudimentary premises at the rear of Dunbar's Corral, some way down Fremont Street from Rance's office. They hardly reflected the income that he could bring in, but in reality he wasn't there very often. The new marshal had given no thought to what he would do if Behan were absent, so it was lucky for him that the building was occupied. He flashed Holliday a meaningful glance and handed over his shotgun.

'Watch my back, please, Doc.' Without awaiting a response, he advanced on the solid wooden door.

As Tombstone's finest crossed his threshold, Johnny Behan looked up from the heavy ledger on his desk. His smooth face was abruptly a picture of conflicting emotions, but the one that finally took precedence was fear. There was something about the grim figure in the black hat that chilled him to the core, but to be fair, he did his level best to recover. Forcing a smile, the county official stood up and optimistically extended a hand. To his dismay, Rance completely ignored him and veered off towards the two iron barred cells at the rear. One contained a sullen and very grimy prisoner, whilst the other was empty; the door open and apparently undamaged.

Cursing the fact that all his deputies were elsewhere, Behan tried again by remarking brightly, 'You must be the new town marshal. I'd heard that Clum had appointed someone. I hope we'll work well together ... if the need arises.'

Rance's only response was to make a careful examination of the iron lock, which left the sheriff beginning to feel distinctly foolish in his own domain. 'Now see here, friend,' he began. 'I'm all for co-operation with a fellow law officer, but you've no ...'

His visitor suddenly rounded on him with eyes blazing. 'From what I hear, Ringo escaped from *your* jail before he even had time to take a shit. Doesn't that seem a bit odd? Especially as there's no sign of any damage and there isn't even a mark on you ... *yet.*'

Behan recoiled from the unexpected tongue-lashing. He had not missed the thinly veiled threat and fervently wished that someone ... anyone would step into his office. He got his wish, but the outcome did little for his rattled nerves.

The door opened and that 'damned lunger' Holliday appeared. 'You need any help with this snake?' that man queried in his distinctively southern drawl.

Rance's expression momentarily softened. 'Be obliged if you'd cover the door. The sheriff's about to tell me where I can find a certain Johnny Ringo. It's known as "co-operation with a fellow law officer",' he added facetiously. Then, without any warning, he launched a massive open-handed slap onto Behan's face. With an anguished yelp, the lawman stumbled back into his swivel chair. The sudden impetus sent that rolling back into the timber wall and rewarded him with a sharp crack to the back of his head.

Rance went after him like a mountain lion after its prey. Seizing Cochise County's finest by his hair, he half-dragged him across the office and slammed him up against the iron bars of the vacant cell. The prisoner in the adjoining cell laughed out loud with unconcealed glee, but the marshal completely ignored him.

'Where's Ringo headed?' he demanded.

Behan was struggling to get his breath, but finally managed to blurt out, 'How the hell should I know?'

The answer to that was far worse than he could have envisaged, as Rance grabbed his head like a melon and smashed it against the unyielding bars. '*Now* you look like there's been a genuine jailbreak.'

As Behan howled with pain and outrage, blood flowed freely from a gash in his head. His tormenter bellowed at him, 'The only woman I've ever loved took a bullet from Ringo's rifle when he should have been locked up in here. I've never before killed in cold blood, but you either give me some answers or you die now … real hard!'

Johnny Behan viewed him through watering eyes the size of saucers. He needed no further convincing. There was a madman on the loose in his office and he just wanted rid of him. Spittle flew from his lips as he blurted out, 'Ringo got word of a big herd of cattle grazing over the border in Sonora. It's too good to miss, what with beef prices going up and up.'

Rance needed more. 'Where in Sonora?'

'Place called Agua Prieta Canyon. It's a perfect spot to keep them corralled … I'm told.'

'I know of it,' piped up Holliday helpfully and with that, the tension in Rance's body began to ease.

41

He stepped back from the cowering lawman, but he wasn't quite finished. 'And shouldn't you as county sheriff be trying to stop rustling? Or isn't catching law breakers part of your duties?'

Despite the sickening pain in his skull, Johnny Behan appeared to be genuinely puzzled. 'What's it to me if some greasers lose their cattle? Mexico's a whole other country. Tombstone's growing by the day and the army always needs food.'

Marshall Toller regarded him pityingly. 'The law's the law! You can't pick and choose which bits of it you enforce. Seems to me you're in the wrong job.' So saying, he turned on his heels and headed for the door.

Holliday was watching him intently, a wry smile playing on his thin lips.

'What?' demanded Rance, who really wasn't in the mood.

The other man heaved the door open. 'Did you really mean all that?'

Stepping out onto the open ground at the rear of the corral, Rance favoured him with the makings of a smile, but his eyes were like chips of ice as he replied.

'No offence, but you must have had a real careless upbringing, Doc. You can't play with the rules when you carry the law. Thing is, when you're facing down some thug with a gun, rules are all you've got to live by. As the years go by, they stop your guts turning to mush.'

As the two men arrived on Fremont Street, myriad thoughts came into Holliday's head. 'This hombre makes Wyatt Earp seem like a slack-jawed yokel. Maybe if I'd hooked up with him sooner my life wouldn't be in such a dang blamed mess. Then again, it's amazing he's lived this long.'

*

Back in the jailhouse, Behan shook his head to clear the ringing in his ears and immediately regretted it. Bile rose into his mouth and he abruptly realized that he was going to be sick. As vomit spewed from his mouth, his sole remaining prisoner regarded him hopefully.

'Any chance of me escaping as well, Mr Behan? Only I'm partial to a bit of rustling myself.'

Any passers-by that knew the sheriff well would have been stunned at the garbled flood of vitriol that emanated from that normally affable man's office. Even as he struggled to rein in his temper, Behan was realizing that he would do well to make himself scarce. Because whatever happened in Sonora, the outcome was unlikely to bode well for him.

Rance Toller was in an itching all-fired hurry to look in on Angie and so it was that he uncharacteristically missed the two cowboys who were on the street and quite blatantly wearing sidearms. However, the newly deputized Doc Holliday did not and he was quick to point out the fact. Whether they were newcomers in town or hard cases deliberately on the prod, mattered little. They needed disarming. It was just very bad timing that they should catch Rance when he had so much on his mind.

'Better let me handle this, Doc. You're not badged up yet.'

With the sun in his eyes, the lawman took advantage of a passing freight wagon to manoeuvre behind the two men. Their spurs and chaps marked them out as new arrivals, but Rance was taking no chances. Gripping the butt of his holstered Remington, he called out, 'Hold on there, fellas. You and I need to parley.'

The two men ambled to a halt and turned to face him. Their grizzled faces registered only mild curiosity. With the sun now strategically in their eyes, it was debatable whether they actually recognized that Rance was a lawman.

'There's a town ordinance that prohibits the carrying of firearms within city limits,' that man explained in language, which to them was hopelessly confusing. It was also pretty obvious that neither of the trail hands gave two hoots what kind of metropolis they were in.

One of the men screwed his eyes up as though it was all just too much. 'There's a which that does what?' he mumbled throatily.

Rance sensed that they were probably harmless, but unfortunately for them his professional calm was only skin deep. Ever since the attack on Angie, he had been consumed by a seething anger that would not tolerate anyone deflecting his purpose, however innocently.

'You're breaking the law, toting those firearms. Hand them over, butts first. *Now!*' he rasped harshly.

Perceiving the sudden danger, one of them hastened to comply and carefully placed a battered Schofield revolver into Rance's left hand. Sadly, the simple one chose belligerence instead.

'You got no call jawing at us like that, mister. We're looking to spend mucho dinero in this shithole.' As he spoke, his unshaven visage flushed with colour and instinctively his right hand closed around the well-worn butt of his revolver.

It was the only provocation that Rance needed. Like a striking rattlesnake, he drew the solidly built Remington and slammed its barrel up against the side of the other's skull. With an anguished cry, that man sank to his knees. Rance tossed the confiscated Schofield over to Holliday and then swiftly bent down to snatch the abruptly untended revolver.

'You had no call to beat on him like that,' protested the injured man's companion, but then instantly regretted it.

With the mild complaint acting more like the caress of a branding iron, Rance traversed his revolver until the muzzle pointed directly at the other's face. 'Either of you fellas got any holdout weapons?' he demanded coldly. 'It'll go badly for you if I have to find them myself.'

As that man stared into the black muzzle of the cocked Remington, beads of sweat erupted over his face. He genuinely couldn't understand how events had turned so nasty so quickly.

'Sweet Jesus, mister. Ease up, will you? We only came into town for some fun. A steak dinner and maybe a crack at one of your whores.'

If he had hoped that that would break the unbearable tension, he was to be sadly disappointed. Rance's trigger finger began to tighten and there was nothing but bitter rage in his eyes. The cowboy could feel his bowels beginning to loosen as the lawman replied.

'I don't run whores and you're plum out of time.'

As even Holliday recognized that things were going too far, the terrified man cried out, 'I've got a knife in my boot and a Winchester in a saddle scabbard over at the Lexington Livery. Pete's got likewise and a Derringer in his jacket, but only 'cause he won it in a card game. Honest, Marshal. We don't mean no trouble.'

The obvious desperate sincerity of the man's words finally registered with Rance. Slowly drawing in a deep breath, he carefully lowered the hammer down onto the lethal centrefire cartridge. Nodding almost to himself, he remarked, 'Your guns will be behind the bar at the Occidental. Check 'em out when you leave Tombstone.'

With that, he abruptly turned on his feet and strode off, leaving one man down and bleeding and the other white and trembling. Holliday favoured them both with a sad smile. Ostentatiously tapping the area where his new badge was to sit, he then took possession of the various weapons before moving off after the troubled lawman. It occurred to the dentist turned 'sporting man' that the town might well benefit from a period of grace, while Rance Toller followed his own particular demons down into Mexico.

CHAPTER FIVE

The five men sat in one of the many offices owned by the Grand Central Mine. The company owned the largest silver mining operation in the San Pedro Valley area, with control of it centred on the town of Tombstone. As if emphasizing this, the sound of heavy machinery provided a permanent background noise to the proceedings. The atmosphere in the room was noticeably strained. Recriminations were in the air and for once in his life Mayor Clum was baffled.

'We needed a town marshal,' he heatedly reminded them. 'And this man Toller prevented Johnny Ringo from robbing the Tucson stage. I would remind you gentlemen that since *your* money was in the Wells Fargo strongbox, he did you a service. There's also the fact that nobody else wanted the damn job. So what more do you want from him, for God's sake?'

A heavyset man in an expensive suit was about to tell him. 'There's no need to get wrathy, John,' he retorted with an ominous frown. 'You know as well as I do that it was actually Wells Fargo's money that he saved, because they cover all losses from robbery. But that's just splitting hairs. I happen to agree with you that we need a lawman, *but* one who knows how to walk soft. By all accounts you've over-reached yourself, *Mayor* Clum. Without conferring with us, you've taken on another hard nose, just like those damned Earp brothers. We don't … *can't* have another bloodbath like the O.K. Corral. It didn't even happen there, but thanks to dime novels and newspapers like yours, the whole country knows about it and that's just plain bad for business. I don't give a damn who kills who, but this territory needs to be *perceived* by the outside world to be peaceful.'

E.B. Gage, Superintendent of the Grand Central, paused to draw breath. Nobody even considered interjecting, because Gage was the nearest thing Tombstone had to a celebrity … as well as being immensely powerful.

'Someone like *you* might not realize it, but it takes a vast amount of money to extract silver ore out of this valley. How can we continue to attract investment if *your* marshal beats seven shades of shit out of everyone he encounters? He's supposed to be a *peace officer*, for Christ's sake!'

John Clum could feel colour coming to his face, but before he could respond another man chipped in. 'This *thug* Toller even attacked the county sheriff in his own office. Just who the hell does he think he is?'

Someone else guffawed delightedly. 'That's no bad thing. That little asshole, Behan, is too full of himself by half.'

Gage had heard enough. 'Maybe so, but he's got political clout as well and I for one want to see Tombstone in the county seat of Cochise County. So this new marshal has to go.' He took another breath and lowered his voice almost to a whisper, but every man in the room heard what he said next. 'Sack him. Pay him off. Or shoot him. I don't care which. Just do something!'

Clum was seething with anger and frustration. He knew that he had little choice, but nevertheless tried one more time. 'That might not be so easy. His woman's laid up in the Grand Hotel, likely to die from Ringo's bullet and Toller's teamed up with Doc Holliday ... the same man that killed Tom McLaury at that *bloodbath* I reported on. And they're both out of town right now, hunting down Ringo.'

That cut no ice with the mining operator. 'Well then, you'd better hope that they never make it back, because one way or another they're both history!'

'Don't take this the wrong way, Doc, but just why are you helping me out like this? Apart from the $3 a day you're getting as my deputy, of course.'

Holliday was on the point of answering, when yet another vicious wracking cough came from nowhere and tore through his emaciated frame. Rance watched with genuine concern as fresh flecks of blood spattered the much-used handkerchief. As the other man struggled to drag air into wasted lungs, he moved off a little way and scrutinized the terrain. Having left Tombstone at first light, the two men had ridden south, paralleling the San Pedro River and taking care to avoid the town of Bisbee. It was a known haunt of the Cowboys and they didn't want word of their presence to reach Ringo and his cronies.

To Rance's untutored eye, the surrounding land appeared to be merely parched and lifeless desert, capable only of supporting the many misshapen cactus that were dotted about. To a man used to the northern states, it seemed like an alien environment and in spite of the heat he shivered. He was sincerely glad to be in the company of someone who knew the territory.

'It can have that effect on you at first,' observed a perceptive and partially recovered Holliday. 'And in answer to your question, I'm helping you in part because I strongly disapprove of violence towards the fairer sex. There aren't enough of them out here that we should want to go shooting holes in them. Johnny Ringo is a scoundrel of the first order and I intend to be there when he is laid to rest.' Then he remembered the tin star now pinned to his chest. 'Or at least until he is safely behind bars.'

Rance smiled appreciatively. He was feeling considerably calmer than the previous day. The knowledge that Angie had been breathing easier when they left had eased his mind and the lack of any miscreants to 'pistol whip' was also helping.

'Just how far off is this canyon?' he enquired.

'Couple more hours should do it. It's only just over the border. There's plenty of grass and water. The Mexicans use it as a staging post to fatten up the cattle before driving them north into the U.S. to get a higher price. Trouble is, the Cowboys know that as well. Could be we just arrive in time to pick up the pieces. There's been mucho blood spilt in Agua Prieta Canyon and I don't reckon the killing will end any time soon.'

After leaving two of their number on the rim as horse holders, the remaining ten Cowboys had continued on foot down to the open end of the box canyon. The bright red sashes endowed them with a colourful quality that was totally at odds with their murderous intent. All the men carried repeating rifles and from past experience they knew it would be like shooting fish in a barrel. *If* they could achieve complete surprise.

In Agua Prieta Canyon, nature had created the perfect corral, but it was also a death trap for those allowing themselves to be cornered inside it. With only one way in or out and containing a small lake fed by spring water, it made controlling a herd of cattle remarkably easy. Unfortunately for the nine vaqueros charged with delivering the herd, the benign conditions had lulled them into a false sense of security. No one had thought to mount a guard on the rim and all of them were imbued with the Mexican tradition of *mañana*: 'tomorrow is always soon enough'.

On John Ringo's signal, the Cowboys eagerly opened up with their repeaters. Their ragged volleys sent a lethal hail of lead tearing into the horrified vaqueros. Sprawled around on the ground at their ease, they had little chance to retaliate. Bullet after bullet ripped through flesh, sometimes finding vital organs and other times breaking bone. As empty brass cartridges piled up at the feet of the *gringos*, great clouds of smoke from the black powder collected in the still air and began to affect their aim. Sadly, it was a case of 'too little too late' to save the blood-spattered Mexicans. The eventual result could only be total annihilation. Close by, the cattle began to stir nervously, but sated by lush grass and plentiful water they failed to stampede.

'Hot dang, will you look at that?' one of the Cowboys yelled out jubilantly. No one had expected so easy a victory and his excitement was heightened by relief.

Ringo remained silent and continued working the action of his Winchester with terrifying efficiency. His eyes were filled with the sick frenzy that always came over him during a killing spree. Indians, Mexicans or even his fellow Americans, it made no odds to him. The only time that he really felt any exhilaration was when he was taking the lives of others.

Finally, there was simply no one left alive to shoot and the gunfire reluctantly petered out. The ten men elatedly advanced on the camp, reloading their weapons on the move. Bullet riddled vaqueros lay everywhere. The Cowboys' one-sided conquest was complete. Ringo hollered up to the rim, ordering the horse holders to get their mounts down there, pronto. The herd of cattle was theirs for the taking and the sooner they got back over the border the better.

'Water the horses and then we're moving out,' he commanded.

'What about robbing the stiffs first?' responded one of his men with obvious disappointment.

'We ain't grubbing about in the dirt for a few *pesos*,' Ringo retorted dismissively. 'That herd's worth a whole heap of gold simoleons and there's no telling who heard all that shooting. I want those beeves on the move, full chisel. That is unless you fancy arguing the toss with a troop of *Rurales*. I didn't escape from one stinking jail just to end up rotting in another!'

His men suddenly glanced uneasily up at the forbidding walls of the canyon, their euphoria fading. No, they didn't fancy that at all. One man did mutter under his breath, 'He's all shit an' no sugar!' but as their two cronies arrived leading all the horses, the Cowboys completely ignored the cadavers and did as their leader instructed. As it turned out, it was that careless error that saved the life of one of the vaqueros!

*

'Somebody's making enough noise to wake snakes,' Holliday colourfully observed.

Rance took a more considered view. 'Which means that whatever *was* going to happen *has* happened. So it would behove us to tread carefully, if we're going to check this out.'

'Well, that's what we came down here for,' wheezed Holiday, taking a drink from a canteen that Rance would have bet a month's wages contained whiskey rather than water. 'I'll lead us in at the highest point overlooking the canyon. That way we won't collide with anything hightailing out of it.'

As it transpired, by the time that they reached it, Agua Prieta Canyon appeared to be totally devoid of life. In fact, on closer inspection through the marshal's drawtube spyglass, it looked more like a butcher's yard. And whatever cattle had been in it were gone, but all the tracks were fresh.

'We'd better water the horses before we head out after them,' remarked Rance grimly.

'Oh, there's no fired hurry,' Holliday responded confidently. 'You see, I happen to know exactly where they're going. Back over the border there's a…'

He suddenly lost his audience as Rance sat bolt upright. 'Down there by the pool. Something moved!'

A bloodstained hand clawed at the sky and this time both men saw it. 'Looks like Ringo's losing his touch,' replied the southerner, but he drew his revolver anyway.

The two men rode their horses around and down to the open end of the canyon before dismounting. Then, weapons at the ready, they cautiously advanced on foot, all the time scanning their surroundings for any sign of a trap. Bullet riddled vaqueros lay all around and it soon became obvious that there was only the one survivor.

'*Agua!*' that man croaked pathetically.

Finally satisfied that there was no immediate danger, the two men crouched down next to him. The Mexican's shirt was drenched with blood and his eyelids were flickering feebly. A cursory examination was enough for Holliday. 'Gut shot. He won't last the hour.'

'*Agua, por favor.*'

The poor soul was obviously desperately thirsty and Rance quickly recovered the canteen from his saddle. His companion had apparently lost interest, because he had wandered off to scrutinize the other victims of the massacre. In his right hand he gripped something black and metallic, but the marshal gave little thought to its purpose as he bent over the Mexican and gently cradled his head. As water trickled into the dying man's mouth, Rance was rewarded with a weak smile.

'Easy, friend. Easy,' he responded. 'Let's see if I can make you a bit more comfortable.' So saying, he glanced around for the man's hat to use as a pillow. As he did so, he unexpectedly caught sight of Holliday's scrawny figure grotesquely straddling a corpse. His deputy appeared to be strangely exerting himself and he suddenly became aware of a creaking sound. Although the noise was vaguely familiar, something about the bizarre tableau sent a shiver up his back.

'What the hell are you up to, Doc?' he demanded brusquely.

Doc's right arm jerked back sharply and then he turned to favour Rance with a disarming smile. Even as he did so, he held up his right hand to display a pair of dripping pliers. In their brutal grip was a freshly extracted tooth, complete with a chunk of bloodied gum.

'Sweet Jesus, what are you about?' Rance persisted uneasily.

Holliday was not in the slightest bit flustered. 'Once a dentist, always a dentist. A decent set of teeth'll fetch good money back East, for dentures and such, and these unfortunates no longer have need of theirs.' With that, he dropped the gruesome object into the crown of his hat and set to work on another.

Rance was dumbfounded. To his rather prudish mind, such behaviour was only one step up from grave robbing. He was about to protest, when his attention was suddenly taken by something far more alarming. The ground abruptly trembled under the impact of many hoofs and without any other warning, a large group of horsemen swept into the canyon. With consummate skill they seized the Americans' horses and then spread out around their two owners. In the face of such numbers, Rance wisely kept his hands well clear of any weaponry and despite his pounding heart, he forced himself to calmly scrutinize the newcomers. To a man they wore grey jackets with silver braid, wide sombreros and a mixture of red or black neckties. All were heavily armed with carbines, sabres and revolvers, and it was the latter that they appeared about to use.

One man out in front, chewing on a stubby cheroot, seemed to be the leader. His hard eyes first took in Rance, as he squatted next to the dying vaquero and then settled ominously on Doc Holliday. With his pliers quite literally locked onto a large back molar, the former dentist was in a desperately incriminating position and it was more than enough for the visibly incensed Mexican. Cocking his six-gun, he spat out of the corner of his mouth prior to uttering two words. '*Gringo* assassins!'

As the revolver lined up on him, Holliday dropped his pliers and went for his own weapon. It was a futile gesture and he knew it, but the gunfighter and cardsharp was game to the end.

'No, *jefe*!' The words came from a most unexpected quarter and were sufficient to make the Mexican hold fire. His mortally wounded countryman made a supreme effort and rattled off some rapid fire Spanish, all the while gesturing up at Rance, before finishing weakly with, '*Por favor.*' Then, exhausted by the exertion, he lay still.

Holliday had had the sense to freeze and recognizing this, the leader held up his hand to restrain his men. The American muttered out of the corner of his mouth, 'They're *Rurales*. Mexican police.'

Keeping his hands in plain sight, Rance slowly turned towards the horsemen and pointed at the badge visible on his chest. 'I am a lawman from Tombstone, Arizona,' he stated, speaking slowly and clearly. He had no idea how much American they understood, but it was worth a try. 'I am pursuing a fugitive. The same outlaw that killed these people.'

The travel-stained *Rurale* stared at him long and hard before apparently reaching a decision. Nodding thoughtfully, he then gestured at Holliday. 'And him. What is his purpose?'

Rance theatrically shrugged and blew through his nose like a horse as he tried to think of something that made sense in the circumstances. Finally he simply replied, 'He's a dentist.'

The Mexican's eyebrows raised momentarily, before the makings of a smile flickered across his dusty features. Looking pointedly down at Holliday, he remarked, 'It pleases me to allow you to continue with your work … for now.' So saying, he briskly dismounted and all his men save one followed suit. That unfortunate was sent up onto the rim to stand guard.

As his men eagerly led their mounts to water, their leader approached Rance who had by now got to his feet. 'I am Capitan Rodriguez of the *Guardia Rural*. You may know of us as the *Rurales*. You realize that wretch saved your lives?'

Rance glanced down at the ashen features of the dead vaquero. 'And I'm very grateful, but sadly for him, it was the last thing he did.' Extending his right hand, he added, 'I'm Marshal Rance Toller. That man over yonder is my deputy. When he's not pulling teeth, that is.' He deliberately avoided supplying Holliday's name in case his dubious reputation had travelled below the border.

After accepting his handshake, the *Rurale* stepped back to beat the dust from his uniform. With the two Americans no longer in mortal danger, Rance took his first proper look at the Mexican. Capitan Rodriguez was short and stocky and definitely less intimidating afoot. And yet, he definitely carried about him an air of authority. The twin bandoleers of ammunition that were draped crossways over his chest reinforced this, as did the way his men hurried to comply with his orders. The question was, how did he intend to deal with the two trespassing northerners? They had no jurisdiction in Sonora or indeed even any rights.

'You *gringos* have been coming into my country killing and stealing for years,' Rodriguez suddenly accused. His recent mild manner had entirely disappeared, replaced by that of a snarling despot. Belatedly, Rance noticed that his thin lips had a decidedly cruel aspect to them. 'You are nearly as bad as the cursed Apaches! Tell me why I shouldn't just shoot you anyway and leave your bodies here as a warning to others.'

The capitan was clearly on the prod and waiting to see how one particular *gringo* would respond. Rance decided to follow a hunch and dispense with any pussyfooting about. Drawing himself up to his full height, he retorted, 'I'm a lawman in pursuit of a fugitive. I've never killed anybody that didn't need killing and I don't steal! The men who did this are rustlers led by a gunhand, name of Johnny Ringo. Back in Tombstone he shot my lover, so I want him real bad.'

The marshal paused for a moment. He had spotted a flicker of recognition at the mention of Ringo's name. A crazy idea suddenly came into his head.

'Why don't we work together? My partner with the pliers over there reckons he knows where those murdering sons of bitches are headed. Once we catch up with them, you get to keep the cattle and anyone you haven't killed … except Ringo. He's mine!'

Rodriguez rocked back on his heels slightly. It appeared that he definitely hadn't expected a proposition like that. Then again, he hadn't dismissed it out of hand either. He contemplatively stroked a bushy moustache, before breaking into a smile. 'Your idea has its charms, but surely you must understand that I and my men cannot possibly invade the United States.'

Rance matched the other man's smile. It occurred to him that Rodriguez was either a fine play-actor or disturbingly mercurial. 'You wouldn't be invaders. Once over the border you'd be part of my posse and under my orders.'

The capitan considered the implications of that. Such co-operation had never happened before, but that didn't mean it couldn't succeed. And being with a Yankee lawman would prove very interesting indeed in the event of them encountering any U. S. Cavalry patrols. He grabbed the cheroot from his mouth and laughed out loud at the thought. 'You have a deal, *señor*. If you really want it.'

Rance glanced over at his deputy. Holliday was greedily wrenching bloodied teeth out of yet another corpse. Some sixth sense told him that the man's efforts could well turn out in vain. As he thoughtfully returned his attention to the Mexican officer, his response was far more low key. 'I reckon so.'

CHAPTER SIX

Daybreak the following morning saw the combined force preparing to leave Agua Prieta Canyon. As Rance made up his bedroll, Holliday moved some distance away from the main party and began to cough and spit as though it was going out of fashion. Rodriguez glanced over at the marshal quizzically.

'It takes him a while to get the phlegm situated,' Rance offered by way of explanation, but it was insufficient for the capitan.

'Just what is it that ails that man?' he persisted.

'Consumption,' Rance replied. 'It's very slowly killing him.'

The *Rurale* nodded coolly, but made no further comment.

A short while later, as the men mounted up, Rodriguez urged his horse over to where Holliday was tightening the cinch strap around his own animal. The capitan had three *Rurales* at his back and that alone was enough to put Rance, observing from the sidelines, on edge.

'You hold many teeth that do not belong to you, deputy. I would have them now, *por favor.*'

Holliday peered up at the Mexican in amazement. Then his eyes narrowed as he took in the other man's set expression. Realizing what was happening, his unnaturally pale features began to register belligerence and he slowly pulled the frock coat clear of his holstered revolver.

'I don't recall poking around in your mouth, Captain. So I reckon I'll just hang on to what's mine by right of possession.'

Rodriguez motioned to his men and they fanned out next to him. 'Those teeth belonged to my countrymen, *señor*. You are not from Mexico, so it is only right that I should have them. Besides, I understand that you are not long for this world and then they would only go to waste, *si*?'

Rance's hand closed over the breech of his shotgun. The situation had unaccountably turned very ugly very quickly. He knew that the other *Rurales* had him covered, but he couldn't just abandon Holliday to his fate. In a sea of unsmiling faces, a knife could have cut the tension and everything suddenly hinged on the dentist's response.

In the past it had seemed to more than a few onlookers that John Holliday had a death wish and to some extent they would have been correct, but he was always protective of the very few friends that he had made. As the *Rurales* closed around him, he was aware of Rance clutching the sawn-off and he felt a warm glow in the pit of his gut. Not in any way would he deliberately risk that man's life purely for personal gain. And so it was that he allowed the frockcoat to fall forward over his sidearm. With a rueful grin that entirely failed to reach his eyes, he passed a blood-stained cotton pouch filled with freshly extracted teeth up to the capitan.

'What the hell,' he remarked lightly. 'Easy come, easy go.

They don't amount to much anyway.'

As Rodriguez reached down to accept the offering, his mood changed yet again and his dark features were suddenly wreathed in smiles. 'A wise decision, *señor*. We can now cross the border as friends, *sí*?' Without awaiting a response, he waved at his men and cried out, 'Come, *muchachos*, let's ride. We have many *gringo* sons of bitches to kill.'

Winking broadly at Tombstone's marshal, the capitan led his men out of the box canyon and off towards the Arizona border. Above them, carrion birds impatiently circled, eager to begin feasting. Rance heaved a great sigh of relief and clambered up into his saddle. Walking his horse over to Holliday, he remarked, 'Jesus, you cut it fine, Doc. Those fellas are more like bandits than lawmen.'

Holliday grunted. 'That's probably because many of them are. If they get captured, they join the *Rurales* so as to avoid a Mexican prison. Believe me, you'd do the same.' Mounting up, he too winked broadly at his companion. 'Besides, they were just joshing with me. If they'd killed me, they wouldn't know where to find Ringo and the cattle.'

Rance stared at him in total disbelief, but decided against making anything of it. Mention of Ringo reminded him that he didn't know where they were headed either. 'So just where are we all going, anyhow?'

As the two men spurred off in pursuit of their temporary collaborators, Holliday replied, 'I'm almost certain that we'll find those murdering varmints on the Clanton spread. I've had dealings with that family before. In fact, earlier this year, I helped Wyatt Earp and his brothers kill young Billy Clanton. Whilst upholding the law, of course!' Then, as though such things were entirely normal, he added conversationally, 'He was only nineteen, you know.'

Rance Toller's eyes widened with surprise and under his breath he muttered, 'That's just marvellous!'

A conscience was a bad thing for a newspaper proprietor to possess and John Clum was seriously struggling with his. Very little that went on in Tombstone escaped his attention and it was because of this that he slowly and extremely reluctantly made his way over to the Grand Hotel. There was far more on his mind than Angie Sutter's current condition, but that would do for a start.

Angie had spent a reasonably comfortable night alone in her room. Even out on the rough and ready frontier, unless she was a common whore, it would have been unseemly for Drew Williams to spend the night innocently watching over her from the rocking chair. And in truth she *was* on the mend. So when there came a tap on the door, she presumed that it was merely the Wells Fargo agent looking in on her. As the Mayor of Tombstone stepped hesitantly across the threshold, her surprise was plain to see.

'Sorry to trouble you, missus … miss … er, may I call you Angie?'

His discomfort was obvious, but at that stage she didn't have any inkling as to what was really behind it. So she chuckled lightly and then instantly regretted it as a sharp pain lanced through her left shoulder.

'Angie'll do fine, Mr Clum,' she finally managed, 'and yes, I am on the mend, although it doesn't do for me to try moving around too much.'

He stood looking at her awkwardly for a moment or two, until the young woman decided that she'd best help him to the point. 'So, what can I do for you, *Mr Mayor*? Or are you here on behalf of the Tombstone *Epitaph* to pay me for my story in freshly minted silver dollars?'

Her flippancy produced something approaching anger, because in truth he considered that he was putting himself at some risk by even being there. 'If I had half the sense I was born with I wouldn't be stood here,' he retorted heatedly. Then he got a grip on his emotions and tried again. 'You and Rance seem akin to decent people. Too good for a boomtown like Tombstone, really.' He paused momentarily and then the floodgates opened. 'Rance has shown himself to be too good at his job. Way too good. The people who really hold the power hereabouts want him gone. They told me to get rid of him … by any means. Trouble is they obviously don't consider me to be the real McCoy, because the mine superintendent, E.B. Gage, has bought himself some insurance.'

Angie was mystified and showed it.

'A newspaper man sees everything,' he elaborated. 'There are half a dozen newcomers suddenly arrived in town who just don't look right. Tied down guns and hard stares. They're certainly not prospectors and they look too clean to be rustlers. I reckon they're Gage's insurance, if you know what I mean.'

Oh, she knew what he meant all right, but before Angie could make any comment he was off again, albeit without any sign of logical thought. 'If I was you I'd make myself scarce, because they'll know all about you. Head south out of town and then wait for Rance to reappear. With or without Ringo makes no difference. The pair of you can just turn him loose if necessary and hightail it out of Cochise County. Better still, get out of Arizona entirely.'

She stared mutely at him in disbelief for a few moments. Despite or possibly because of the pain in her shoulder, she could feel real anger building up inside. Angie had never been slow to speak her mind and this occasion wasn't going to be any different.

'You must have rocks for brains, *Mr* Mayor! You encouraged us to settle here in the first place. I got shot in *your* town because Rance did his duty as a man. If I try to ride anywhere, I'll get this shoulder bleeding again and that'll finish what Ringo started. Besides which, even if I could go out there and find him, Rance wouldn't just up and leave. He doesn't run from anyone. I reckon you're running scared and just trying to cover your own ass!'

John Clum had never been talked to in such a way by a *mere* female, even a damned attractive one. His face flushed red and he took a step towards the sick bed. At that moment there was a perfunctory tap on the door and Drew Williams walked in. He had overheard Angie's raised voice and was shrewd enough to realize that it was time for the mayor to leave.

'Morning, John,' he conversationally remarked. 'The marshal's not going to be pleased if he finds out that you've been tiring my patient.'

Guiltily, Clum spun around and peered wordlessly at the newcomer, but Angie hadn't quite finished. 'You invited us to stay, so you'll have to see it through with us. It's called consequences. Now get out!'

Without even a backwards glance, he did exactly that. His undignified flight brought a fleeting smile to her pale features, but she was uncomfortably aware that the trouble that he had brought with him would not be so easily dismissed.

*

Blissfully unaware of the ominous turn of events in Tombstone, Marshal Rance Toller had just been informed by his deputy that they were now most definitely back in Arizona Territory. On his own initiative they spurred their animals forward, moving past the column of *Rurales* and taking their rightful place at its head. On the face of it, Capitan Rodriguez genially acknowledged this display of authority, but his dark features soon resumed the brooding intensity that was familiar to his men.

As they drew ever closer to their destination, Rance sought to take advantage of Holliday's local knowledge. 'Who are these Clantons and what can we expect from them, Doc?'

That man finally pocketed the kerchief that he had been holding to his mouth since leaving camp. The effects of 'eating' the Mexicans' dust had been causing him severe problems.

'There aren't as many of them as there used to be,' he remarked drolly. 'Billy met his end in Tombstone and Old Man Clanton stopped several bullets in a Mexican reprisal raid … a little bit like the one you're leading. That leaves Phin and Ike. Phin's the elder by two years, but I don't know much about him. Ike's the one to watch out for. He's a blowhard, a braggart and a cowardly back shooter all rolled into one. Not to mention a passable drunkard.'

'Lovely,' commented Rance dryly. 'So who'll actually be in charge when we come up on them?'

'Oh, Ringo. Without a doubt,' came the immediate response. 'Everyone walks softly around him.'

'Not any longer!'

*

'You might have warned me you were coming,' he whined petulantly.

John Ringo regarded the florid-faced individual scornfully. He had little regard for Ike Clanton, but the location of his ranch came in undeniably useful. 'Well, we're here now, so stop your fussing.'

The rancher stared angrily at him through drink sodden eyes. He had a genuine grievance, but for a moment he couldn't recall just what it was. Then it came to him.

'This just ain't fair. Them's Mexican beeves. The last herd of cattle stolen from Sonora got my pa shot to pieces.'

Ringo took a step towards him. The flesh over his cheek bones seemed to tighten as he hissed dangerously, 'Don't press me, Ike, or you might just end up like him. Besides, who said anything about them being stolen?'

Ike Clanton was flummoxed. 'Huh? Well, whose are they then?'

Ringo was unusually well educated for a frontier gun thug, a fact that he demonstrated in his answer. 'All the owners are deceased. We're kind of acting as executors to arrange their disposal. Now you take another sup at that bug juice while I have a look around.'

Ike, none the wiser, grunted and staggered away into another room. He'd had a belly full of John Ringo already, but even in his drunken state he recognized that he wasn't the man to throw him out.

As his unwelcome guest glanced around the interior of the ranch house, that man's nose twitched with distaste. It hadn't improved any since his last visit. The building was of a very basic clapboard construction, barely strong enough to stop a bullet. Dirt floors and a lack of basic hygiene meant that the place stank. But it was shelter of a kind and it allowed he and his men the chance to rest up for a night before moving further north. It was just a shame that Newman 'Old Man' Clanton had got himself slaughtered, because in addition to dominating his wastrel sons, he had been a pragmatic businessman.

As the Cowboys each staked a claim on an area to flop, one of them happened to glance through an open window.

'Which silly bastard took a sombrero off of those greasers?'

Ringo glanced sharply at the speaker and as he did so a shocking tingle of comprehension travelled the length of his lean frame. Even as he threw himself to the ground, he was simultaneously drawing a revolver and shouting a warning.

'Everybody down!'

As a ragged fusillade of shots rattled out around the ranch house, the thin planking was struck by a variety of lethal projectiles and some of them had enough velocity behind them to keep on going. Not all of the Cowboys possessed their leader's sharp reactions and that was to be their undoing. Disfigured soft lead bullets struck two of them and immediately the sweaty interior resounded to their piercing screams.

'Get those God damn shutters closed,' Ringo bellowed, wisely remaining on the floor. His men knew him of old, however, and completely ignored him. More shots rang out from every direction and as vicious splinters of wood flew about the room, it was obvious that the ranch house was completely surrounded.

Befuddled by cheap whiskey, Ike Clanton lurched into

view from another room and stared around at the prone Cowboys in amazement. He held a Colt in one hand and a chipped keg of 'rot gut' in the other. Completely unfazed by the anguished shrieks of the blood spattered wounded, he called out, 'Who all's doing that shoo … shoo … shooting?'

Ringo didn't even spare him a glance. Instead he crawled over to the window and bellowed out, 'Hold fire, for Christ's sake! Whoever's out there, you've got no call to be shooting. That herd's bought and paid for and I've got paper to prove it.'

The gunfire slackened off and a strangely familiar voice hollered back. 'I couldn't give two shits about your damn cows. It's the *coward* John Ringo that I'm after.'

Ringo blinked rapidly as he absorbed the totally unexpected response. It suddenly came to him just who was out there and he shook his head in surprise. 'You're a persistent son of a bitch, I'll give you that, but you don't have any jurisdiction out here.'

'So I'll make a citizen's arrest,' Rance shouted back. 'And it'll go badly for you if you resist. Because I forgot to mention, there's a troop of *Rurales* out here who *do* want all the cows back *and* a piece of every God damn one of you!'

Before Ringo could even think of a rejoinder to that, another volley from the Mexicans' carbines smashed into the flimsy ranch house. Pots and pans leapt up into the air and one of the window shutters broke free and collapsed into the dirt. One of the wounded men, his chest horribly torn by a piece of disfigured lead, howled out like a baby for his ma. Although nobody else was hit, it was obvious that their situation was untenable. Even Ike had sobered up enough to feel sorry for himself.

'They're blasting my house all to hell,' he whined. 'I don't deserve any of this!'

'Deserve's got nothing to do with it,' responded Ringo scornfully. 'But I'll allow we've got trouble. Likely they'll torch the place next and then we're really for it.' Glancing around at his fellow rustlers, he announced, 'Reckon we'll have to make a break for it, boys. Every man for himself. Those that get clear head for Contention. But first we'd better give those festering law dogs something to think on.'

Capitan Rodriguez knew exactly what needed to be done next. 'We should burn the *gringo* bastards out.' Glancing over at Rance, he offered a vaguely apologetic shrug. 'No offence, *señor.*'

Rance regarded him through narrowed eyes. 'None taken. But just remember, Ringo's mine.'

The Mexican abruptly abandoned any attempt at civility. 'We might be in Arizona,' he snarled. 'But don't ever presume to give me orders.'

At that very moment, Ringo proved that he was far from just a mindless thug. Simultaneously two whiskey jugs, the necks crammed with burning rags, were flung out of windows at either side of the front door. Hitting the hard ground, they shattered and their contents instantly ignited in a spectacular flare-up.

Taken by surprise, the half dozen or so *Rurales* covering the front involuntarily flinched and backed off, which was exactly what Ringo had counted on. Leaving Ike to his own devices, the ten uninjured Cowboys burst out of doors and windows on all sides, guns blazing. Two of those *Rurales* taken by surprise at the front were struck down, before their comrades recovered and returned fire. Outgunned and in the open, Ringo had no intention of trading shots with the Mexicans. He and his few cronies raced for their horses tethered near the cattle. Even as they ran, one of them took a bullet squarely between the shoulder blades and collapsed without a sound.

Those Cowboys at the rear fared far worse. They emerged from cover straight into a disciplined carbine volley that tore bloody holes in them. Two, three, then four men went down coughing blood and twitching in agony. The remaining survivor didn't even try to fight back. He just ran, pell mell after his friends.

Frighteningly oblivious to the carnage around him, Rance had eyes only for John Ringo. Prepared for close combat, his Winchester wasn't to hand, so he levelled his Remington at the fleeing figure and took careful aim. The revolver crashed out and through the haze of powder smoke, he watched his victim stumble and fall. Elation surged through him. With the gunman dead, all he and Holliday had to do was cut loose of the *Rurales* and head back to Tombstone. Hard experience should have told him that life just could not be that simple.

CHAPTER SEVEN

Two things happened simultaneously. John Ringo painfully rolled over prior to sitting up and the nervous cattle finally began to move. Even though tired from the trail, the burning scrub and crashing detonations had them thoroughly spooked. It was lucky for the warring parties that they were not in the path of the stampede. As it was, the simple beasts picked up speed and instinctively headed south, back to the last good water. The *Rurales* had a simple choice. They could either continue slaughtering the *gringos* or they could go after the money.

Capitan Rodriguez could only watch impotently as his men leapt into their saddles and streamed off in pursuit of the cows. 'You poxy sons of whores. I'll have you all flogged,' he bellowed after them, but in his heart he knew that in their place he would probably have done the same.

The four Cowboys still on their feet saw their profit disappearing and their leader down and bleeding. The Mexican captain and the skinny American in the black frock coat were still shooting at them and they simply lost their nerve. 'The hell with this,' yelled one of them. 'I don't fight for free!' With that, they all made a grab for the nearest saddled horses and hightailed it north.

Rance was only vaguely aware of all this because he was grimly advancing on Ringo with the fixed purpose of taking his life. Never before had he been so oblivious of personal danger, but then he had never been in love before either. The gun thug had been hit in his left shoulder, in almost the exact same position that he had struck Angie. Although bleeding heavily and in great pain, he still attempted to level his revolver.

Rance leapt forward, kicking out at Ringo's right hand. That man's Colt Army discharged into the earth and then fell from numbed fingers. 'I should have finished you in Tombstone, law dog,' snarled the Cowboy, his lips twisting in agony.

'And now you'll *never* get the chance,' the lawman rasped as he none too gently placed the muzzle of his Remington on Ringo's forehead. The hammer was cocked. All it needed was a gentle squeeze. His defenceless victim was sweating badly, but somehow he knew that its cause wasn't fear. And then Ringo's last two words repeated in his mind. '*Law dog.*'

'God damn it all to hell,' Rance muttered. Ever so slowly, he eased the hammer down. He just couldn't do it. Killing in cold blood went against everything that his life had been about, as a law *man*.

As the muzzle left his forehead, Ringo sneered up at him. Eerily mirroring his thoughts, he taunted, 'Just couldn't do it, huh?'

Fresh anger flared up within him and Rance jabbed his revolver sharply forward. The muzzle rammed into Ringo's wounded shoulder, causing him to cry out in pain and bringing tears to his eyes. 'Maybe not, but I've given you exactly what you gave Angie. Which makes it an eye for an eye, a tooth for a tooth. So you'd better pray awful hard that she doesn't die!'

As his fury subsided, his senses began to register activity around him and when a single shot rang out behind, Rance swung about in alarm. Before him he found Capitan Rodriguez back in the saddle and off to that man's side lurked Doc Holliday, still on foot. The temporary deputy held a smoking six-gun and sported a satisfied smile, whilst the *Rurale* seemed strangely inanimate. For long moments the Mexican just sat there, his huge sombrero perched precariously on his head, until slowly at first he slid sideways off his horse and down into the dust. Blood flowed over the parched earth and as the ubiquitous cheroot slipped from his lips, it was obvious that he was quite dead.

'Jesus Christ, Doc! What have you done?' Rance exclaimed. 'He was a lawman.'

Holliday was completely unrepentant. 'He was a thief is what he was and he had it coming.' With that he dropped to his knees and eagerly retrieved the pouch of teeth from the dead man's pocket.

Despite the relentless throbbing torment in his shoulder, Ringo managed to produce a grating laugh. 'Ha, don't look so shocked, law dog. That's just what you'd expect from a vicious little cardsharp.'

Holliday casually glanced over at the wounded Cowboy. 'Hello again, Johnny. It has to be said, you've looked better.'

Rance looked from one to the other in surprise. 'You two know each other?'

His deputy huffed. 'Our paths have crossed on occasion. I'll tell you now that ...'

Before he could finish, a thumping noise came from the bullet riddled ranch house. Both lawmen levelled their weapons, but there was other business that had to be attended to before they could investigate.

'Keep me covered while I frisk this one for hold outs, Doc,' Rance commanded. So saying, he patted Ringo down and retrieved a derringer and a wicked looking skinning knife. 'You go loaded for bear, don't you?' he remarked. Then, ignoring the painful protests of his prisoner, he secured a set of manacles around his wrists. 'Just to be on the safe side. And don't even think about running, because you'll surely bleed to death if you try it!'

Together the two lawmen advanced on the ranch house. Noises like the sound of struggling continued to emanate from within. With his blood no longer up, fear of the unknown began to gnaw at Rance's guts. His job never seemed to get easier with the passage of time. Desperately uneasy about just what awaited him, he picked up the remains of one of the shattered kegs and handed it to his companion. 'Heave this through the window and then wait for my all clear.'

Holliday's compliance was followed by a crash inside. The marshal kicked hard at the door and then leapt across the threshold. With all the window shutters open, the unpleasant interior was flooded with light. What Rance saw made him sick to his stomach. A grubby, ill-kempt individual was kneeling on the chest of a wounded man, one hand clamped over that unfortunate's mouth. His other was delving deep into a pocket, doubtless in search of valuables. The helpless victim just had sufficient strength remaining to kick out at the rudimentary furniture.

Rance had disapproved of his deputy's mercenary activities, but at least *his* prey had been dead. Snarling with anger, the lawman bounded forward and viciously pistol-whipped the scavenger across his left cheek. With a howl of pain, that man toppled sideways and lay writhing on the dirt floor holding his face.

'You may as well enter this shithole, Doc, but there's no good news in here.'

Holliday sauntered in and glanced around at the mayhem. 'That's Ike Clanton you've just laid low. I'm guessing he deserved it. He usually does.'

The prostrate rancher glanced up at him with a shock of recognition. His eyes were mean, bloodshot and temporarily watering from the painful gash in his cheek. 'I'm entitled to whatever they've got,' he blustered. 'It's my place and I never invited them here.'

'God knows how you treat invited guests then,' Rance retorted sarcastically. 'Either way, this place is a known haunt of rustlers, so we're torching it before we leave.'

Ike Clanton uttered a howl of indignation and staggered to his feet. He took in the badges of office and hesitated slightly whilst collecting his thoughts. 'That's not a county badge. You're not one of Behan's men so you've got no say out here, you son of a bitch.' He paused and then added as an afterthought, 'Just who the hell are you anyway?'

Rance had heard enough. He purposefully advanced until he was almost nose-to-nose with Ike and jabbed the Remington's muzzle under that luckless individual's chin. 'I'm the man that's going to raise this piss pit to the ground. If you want to contest that, now's your chance, otherwise *step aside*!'

Ike stared into eyes that were iron hard and unyielding. Quite simply, they were the eyes of a killer and they uncomfortably reminded him of a bruising encounter with another marshal called Wyatt Earp, just before that blood fest in Tombstone. He tried to swallow, but the weapon just wouldn't allow it.

'Christ, he's gonna blow my head off,' he decided. 'OK, OK,' he whined. 'Do what you want. Just let me get a few things together first.' As the revolver was withdrawn, he took a quick look around. 'Jesus, there isn't even any whiskey left. Those bull turds burnt the lot. It just ain't fair what happens to me.'

Rance gazed at him with utter contempt and then turned away. 'I'd be obliged if you'd take a look at the wounded, Doc. See who's fit to travel and who isn't. I don't want to linger too long, in case some of those *Rurales* come back looking for their captain.'

Holliday glanced at him sharply, but his only response was a dry cough before going about his business. There were two survivors inside and possibly some others out back. Rance gratefully left the squalid ranch house and carefully scanned the horizon before rounding up some horses. By the time he had finished, Holliday was ready to report.

'I reckon there's two able to travel and two more that'll just have to bleed out … unless you want to waste some cartridges.'

Rance sighed. 'Which means three wounded prisoners to get back to Tombstone. It's going to be a slow trip. We'd better patch them up and then get the cadavers into the house. Cremation's all they're good for.'

Holliday looked doubtful. 'You right sure that you want

such a big fire? It could pull in some Apaches and we've got enough trouble right now.'

Rance's jaw line tightened. 'I told your friend Clanton that I was going to burn this hovel down and that's exactly what I'm going to do!'

Holliday stared at him reproachfully. 'He's not someone I would ever consider a friend. And I'm not exactly flush with them.'

The marshal peered hard at him for a long moment and then sighed. 'Sorry, Doc. I do run my mouth kind of reckless sometimes. Angie, God bless her, gives as good as she gets and so should you.'

'I'll bear that in mind and I'll tell her you said so. It'll be good to see the lady again.'

The ice was broken and the two men smiled warmly, before turning to the bloody business at hand.

Drew Williams was far from being a brave man. As the local Wells Fargo agent, he was more concerned with timetables and freight charges than gunplay. If 'road agents' caused problems, he left such matters to the company's special trouble-shooters or the local lawmen. Yet, observing Angie's acute mental anguish at the news that one of Gage's regulators had just left town heading south, he had to admit that the sight was tearing him up inside. When he had accepted the role of temporary guardian it had never occurred to him that he would develop feelings for the attractive young lady, but that was exactly what had happened. In the absence of Rance's sobering presence he had fallen for her. So much so that he had come to a momentous decision.

'If it'll make you feel better, I've agreed with myself that

I'll follow that character to see what he's up to. And if I can meet up with Rance, I'll warn him of what awaits him in Tombstone. How's that sound?'

Angie was sitting up in bed. Her shoulder ached abominably, but it was also itching, which was a sure sign that the wound was gradually healing. As the significance of his offer dawned on her, the worry that had been etched into her features lifted slightly and she suddenly favoured him with a dazzling smile.

'You'd do that for me?' she asked, as relief flooded through her body. 'It does sound mighty dangerous.'

Knowing full well what he had just committed himself to, Williams sighed. Yeah, he was most definitely smitten by the young lady before him and it would probably have served his cause better to leave Marshal Toller to whatever fate held for him, but sadly he had been born with an unfortunate curse. He possessed scruples and a notion of what was right.

'Yes,' he replied hoarsely and then added in a firmer voice. 'Yes, I would. And so, much as I'd like to linger here, I'd better make a move. We need to exchange weapons. That long gun of yours will serve me better out in the open. You keep this Colt of mine hidden under the bed sheets. If one of those hired guns should come looking, you parole him to Jesus, you hear?'

Angie Sutter nodded grimly. It wouldn't be the first time that she'd had to kill another human being. 'Oh, I hear you all right. And Drew, thank you.'

As he placed his revolver next to her on the bed, Angie's hand covered his for a moment. The contact was brief, but it was enough to send him striding out of the bedroom feeling a foot taller.

*

'Where's Clanton?' Rance demanded.

His deputy shrugged. 'How should I know? Gone probably, like you told him.'

'Yeah, but where?'

The two lawmen had heaved eight bodies, a mixture of American and Mexican, into the ranch house. The building resembled a slaughterhouse, but wouldn't be standing for much longer. Their three prisoners, wounds roughly bound, sat their horses in hostile silence. The gaudy sashes around their waists were no longer the only splashes of red on their clothing. Ringo was handcuffed to the saddle horn, whilst the other two had their hands roped together.

Holliday was puzzled. 'What do you care? You wanted rid of him, didn't you?'

Rance pointedly stared at him. 'You said he was a backshooter. What if he's out there somewhere, waiting to shoot *us* in the back?'

Holliday whistled appreciatively. 'I'll say one thing, my friend. Your mind sure has a dark turn to it.'

'It's what's kept me alive,' Rance replied dryly as he extracted a precious Lucifer from its wax container.

The bone-dry Clanton house rapidly became a blazing inferno, although thankfully it produced little smoke. What it did emit was a sickly sweet smell of burning flesh that was enough to turn the strongest stomach.

'Time to leave,' Rance announced. 'We'll keep the prisoners in front of us and avoid high ground wherever possible.'

With that, the five men slowly headed north. All of them were glad to escape the nauseating stink, not least because it could easily attract some very unwelcome visitors. Thankfully for the two remaining Cowboys, they were too far-gone to be bothered by such thoughts. Drenched in their own blood, they lay on lice-ridden blankets near the corral, roll-ups thoughtfully placed between their lips. Neither man had more than a few moments left on God's creation, but if they'd had the benefit of second sight, they would probably have decided that they were far better off where they were!

CHAPTER EIGHT

His cronies knew him only as Horogan. He had never supplied a first name and they had never asked. That he was Irish could never be in doubt to anyone who overheard him. Although currently employed with a group of enforcers by Mr E.B. Gage of the Grand Central Mine, by temperament he preferred to work alone and so he had jumped at the opportunity of a solo mission away from Tombstone. He had never liked towns anyway. In his experience they were stinking, disease-ridden places with foul tasting water.

Horogan was particularly suited to his present task. It required him to patrol open country and hopefully to locate and murder Tombstone's troublesome marshal if that man should return from tracking down a certain Johnny Ringo. He hadn't been told the reason why and he hadn't asked. His lifelong hatred of the law took care of any scruples. In the unlikely event that Toller got past him, it would then be up to the remaining five gun hands to finish the job in town.

To help him in his task, he had a particularly good pair of field glasses taken from a dead army scout who had no further use for them and a grimly efficient man-stopper: a model 1876 Winchester .45-70 rifle. It was with the former that the Irish assassin now picked out the four riders heading north towards him. He was a good few miles south of Tombstone and far enough away from any mining activity for his murderous deeds to remain unobserved.

'Sure an' you're a fine man, Horogan,' he muttered to himself in a strong brogue. 'But are you really after killing four men on the off chance?'

The field glasses had excellent clarity up to a certain range. Unfortunately, because of the flat, open terrain, he could not allow them to get that close without risking discovery. So it was that he only picked out the red sash of the lead rider, but not those following on in that man's dust. Horogan had to make a decision and quickly.

'The devil take it. Dem's rustlers at the very least.'

Dismounting, he tethered his horse to a piece of sagebrush and slid the formidable Winchester out of its saddle scabbard. The feel of that finely crafted rifle and the knowledge of just what it was capable of never failed to excite him. After working the smooth lever action, he raised the ladder sight and then lowered himself carefully to the hard ground. Because his prey were in front of him and moving surprisingly fast, he too had to move fast and in doing so he forgot the cardinal rule for a man in his business. As Horogan concentrated intently on windage and elevation, he failed to give any thought to his back trail!

Drew Williams was sweating profusely as he tentatively led his animal forward. Stalking another human being was an entirely new and terrifying experience. So much so that he was beginning to question the logic of even being there. The memory of Angie's smile and any lustful thoughts rapidly faded as more serious matters took precedence. The sun was reaching its zenith and he felt as though he could almost reach out and touch the other man. Then the 'hired gun' dropped to the ground out of sight and Williams almost passed out with fear.

Trembling despite the warmth, he desperately pondered what to do next. The Wells Fargo agent was actually on the point of mounting his horse to flee. What stopped him was the ghastly realization that the hidden assassin might hear him and switch targets. And so he too ground-tethered his animal and dropped to the dirt, clutching Angie's Winchester.

'Come on, me boyos, just a bit nearer,' the Irishman muttered. 'Old Horogan's gonna send you all to hell and may the devil choke me if I fail!'

The four riders were easily in range of the powerful rifle, but he had to maintain a balancing act. He needed them close enough to ensure four hits, but if he left it too long, they were bound to spot his motionless horse. And then it was time and a grim smile spread across his brutalized features. Hugging the rifle butt into his meaty shoulder, he drew a bead on the nearest rider. Drawing in a partial breath, Horogan abruptly held it and squeezed the trigger. There was a satisfying roar and a cloud of powder smoke erupted from the muzzle.

The four men had been riding fast ever since fleeing the Clanton spread. They had no idea whether they were being tracked by the *Rurales* or not, but their instincts told them to keep heading north. Their animals were tiring rapidly, but they weren't ready to ease off just yet. They just wanted to reach a town, any town. Then the leading Cowboy suddenly caught sight of a lone horse standing motionless in the distance. Startled, he was about to turn to his companions when, without any warning, a bullet struck him full on in his chest with ferocious power and knocked him clean off his mount.

Knowing that he was practically invisible to the approaching men, Horogan chose to ignore the 'fire and move' rule and levered up another cartridge into the breach. The remaining horsemen hadn't had time to react and the smoke wasn't thick enough to hinder him, so he again took aim and fired.

Drew Williams was sorely tempted to just close his eyes and keep his nose pressed into the dirt. Yet the mysterious assassin's murderous exploits proved to be too mesmerizing. *And* if that was Rance Toller's party up ahead, he had to do something and quickly, if only for Angie's sake. Then again it was probably too late already. As another shot crashed out, he literally squirmed with fear and indecision. The borrowed rifle in his clammy grasp seemed almost too hot to touch.

'Christ,' he murmured miserably. 'I've got to do something!'

As a second bullet tore into flesh and blood, the two Cowboys who were still breathing intuitively discarded their bright red sashes and struck out in opposite directions. They had no thoughts of retaliation. The hidden gunman was too good for that. Their only chance was to get out of effective rifle range and so they frantically spurred their weary animals to greater efforts.

Horogan was good and he knew it. It also helped that he happened to love his work and positively thrived on the sulphurous smell of the black powder smoke drifting around him. Excitement built up within him as the two survivors separated. Not unnaturally, the poor fools were trying to make it difficult for him and he rose to the challenge. Shifting to his left, he took careful aim at a rapidly retreating back and fired the powerful Winchester for the third time. His shot was true and the luckless Cowboy coughed blood before toppling sideways out of the saddle.

'Sweet Jesus, but this is fun,' the sharpshooter bellowed out exuberantly, little realizing that he actually had an audience.

The final mark was going to be difficult even for him, but that only added to the allure. Deliberately taking his time, Horogan carefully adjusted the rear ladder sight to compensate for the increased distance and then took careful aim at the galloping horse, that being the larger target. His brow furrowed with concentration as he carefully controlled his breathing. Even as he squeezed the trigger he knew that he'd got it right.

The front legs of the distant animal buckled and it fell violently forward. The luckless rider somersaulted clear over its head. Striking the ground with shocking force, the Cowboy rolled a couple of times and then lay still. Glowing with professional pride, Horogan guffawed loudly and leapt to his feet. Completely unaware of the danger lurking behind him, he pumped up another cartridge in case a kill shot should be necessary.

Drew Williams knew that he had failed Angie and yet the knowledge that her beau was now most likely dead, gave him all the more reason to return to her. The thought of that somehow emboldened him, at least by enough to shoot an unsuspecting man in the back! Gingerly getting to his feet, he levelled Angie's rifle at the assassin's broad shoulders and desperately tried to control the shaking in his hands. As his jubilant victim aimed his own rifle, Williams finally summoned enough nerve to squeeze the trigger. At such close range, even an indifferent shot just couldn't miss. The big man cried out with pain and shock and pitched forward, falling heavily onto the hard ground.

'Oh my, what have I done?' Williams's eyes were like saucers as he observed the expanding blood stain on Horogan's jacket. Nevertheless he was drawn by an irresistible curiosity to examine his prey. Scrambling forward, he found that the sudden activity calmed his nerves, but that didn't last long. As he drew level with the body it suddenly moved.

Yelping with panic, Williams belatedly levered up another cartridge, but he needn't have worried. Horogan's life of killing was over for good. With a final convulsive effort, that man shifted onto his side and peered up at his terrified executioner. With blood trickling from his mouth, he managed three words before expiring. '*Pog mo thoin*!'

The Wells Fargo agent stared at him in total bewilderment. He hadn't the slightest idea what that meant. What he did know was that he was now a man killer and that fact began to play tricks on his mind. A strange feeling of invincibility came over him as he picked up the still warm 1876 Winchester. The rifle made a fine trophy and his possession of the weapon that killed them spurred him on to examine the bodies of Marshal Toller and his companions. Mounting up, he made his way exuberantly over to the nearest cadaver.

Drew Williams's buoyant mood dissipated the moment he clapped eyes on the non-entity before him and it got steadily darker with each new blood-soaked discovery. Who the hell are these fellas, he pondered dismally. Soon there only remained one more to inspect and he had been the last to fall. He approached that one with mixed feelings. Since only one shot had been fired and that at the quite obviously dead horse, there was still the possibility of a lone survivor.

His nervous anticipation was soon quelled. Not only was the last man stone dead from a broken neck, but he was also quite plainly *not* Tombstone's marshal. Williams's violent mood swings now produced a feeling of utter disbelief, closely followed by quaking fear. He had never felt so completely isolated. Even the dead men's saddle horses had disappeared out of sight. Surrounded by unknown corpses, killed apparently at random, he suddenly realized that the shooting could quite easily have attracted any number of renegade Apaches.

Clutching his newly acquired rifle for dear life, Williams frantically scrutinized the surrounding horizon. In the course of that rotation, his eyes feverishly looked to the south and as if by some devilish pre-arrangement, he spotted a single horseman heading towards him.

'Sweet Jesus, what if I'm tortured to death?' he wailed at the lifeless individual at his feet. For long moments his tormented mind was a seething morass of panic. Then he took another look at the approaching apparition and logic began to intrude on his thoughts. He recalled hearing stories from the army scouts who occasionally visited Tombstone. One particularly helpful nugget of advice loomed large. 'You never see an Apache until it's too late.'

Gradually it dawned on him that the lone rider was a white man sporting a very worn 'Boss of the Plains' Stetson hat. Relief flooded over him as he optimistically decided that everything was going to turn out just fine after all!

Ike Clanton really didn't know what to make of the scene before him. A lone white man holding two Winchesters was standing next to a dead horse and its apparently equally dead owner. If his own animal hadn't been played out from sheer exhaustion, he would have veered off to the northwest at speed. As it was, he cautiously edged nearer.

Glancing around, Clanton caught sight of three other bodies, two of which still wore the red Cowboy sash and his blood turned to ice water. And yet, although far from courageous, he possessed a dogged resilience that came from living out on the frontier. Recognizing that it was too late to turn and run, he decided to rely instead on the knowledge that he had a Colt revolver hidden in the waistband behind his back. Keeping his hands in plain sight, the dispossessed rancher finally came face to face with a plainly nervous Drew Williams and his own fear turned to bewilderment.

'Hot dang, but I know you,' he exclaimed. 'You're that fella works for Wells Fargo. Since when did you become a mass murderer?'

Williams had no idea who the new arrival was, but since

he clearly didn't represent a threat, his heightened senses relaxed a little. The two rifles suddenly seemed inordinately heavy and so he allowed the butts to slip to the ground. 'I'll allow that it looks that way,' he responded sheepishly, 'but it was that fella over yonder that did all the killing.'

Clanton's thick brows rose expressively. Without a word, he urged his floundering animal over to Horogan's body. One glance was enough to produce a smile of understanding. Moving over to the assassin's tethered animal, he retrieved the reins and then returned to the Wells Fargo man.

'So he massacred this crew,' Clanton remarked conversationally, 'And then you shot him in the back. Nice. Very nice. Only thing I don't understand, is why?'

Williams misinterpreted the sarcasm and in his relief was overly anxious to please. 'He thought it was Marshal Toller returning. Certain interests in Tombstone want rid of him.'

That tickled Clanton. 'Ha, well isn't that just dandy. I wouldn't object coming to conclusions with that law dog myself.' Mind suddenly made up, he produced his Colt Army and ostentatiously cocked the hammer. 'I want both those long guns *and* your horse. Now!'

Williams was astounded at the sudden turn of events. 'You can't leave me out here unarmed,' he wailed. 'What if some Apaches find me?'

'You won't be unarmed,' Clanton retorted. 'Those stiffs'll all have guns. Only by the time you reach them I'll be long gone … on your horse. Now hand over the reins or I'll pop a cap on you.'

Williams's eyes watered with fear and frustration. He made one last effort. 'But why do you need *two* horses?'

Clanton produced an exaggerated sigh. 'Because I might

need one for my brother, Phin. He's been on a ten day drunk in Tombstone. There's nothing left for us around here now, so it's time to move on and who knows, we might even get lucky and run off with a painted lady.' With that inspiring thought, he levelled his revolver at Williams's head. 'Enough talk. Which will it be?'

Quite remarkably, some seed of defiance began to develop within the Wells Fargo agent. After all, hadn't he just killed his first man? Carefully, he allowed the Winchesters to fall to the ground, as though emphasizing that he didn't represent a threat. 'All right, take the damned horses then,' he snapped back. 'But you'll have to murder me if you want these guns. I shot a man for one of them and the other was a gift from … someone important to me.'

Clanton stared at him in surprise. He hadn't expected any resistance. Chewing his bottom lip reflectively, he suddenly found himself getting bored with the unanticipated standoff. He was wasting valuable drinking time and in truth, face to face killings held little appeal for him.

'Keep the poxy things then, if they mean so much to you. Just keep clear of them until I'm gone, you hear?'

As the former rancher rode off with his two new saddle horses he had a thought. 'Who did that gun thug work for anyway?'

Williams, standing disconsolately by Clanton's exhausted animal replied, 'E. B. Gage of the Grand Central.'

'Ha, that figures,' the other man guffawed. 'I'll have some news to *sell* him then. Seems to me you won't be right popular with certain folks when word gets out. Still can't figure out why you got involved with all this.' With that, he urged his animal forward and then just couldn't resist one further taunt. 'If you let him rest up for a few hours, he should get you back to Tombstone. Ha ha ha!'

Williams stared glumly at the wreck of a horse that Clanton had left with him. His only consolation was that he had retained his firearms. 'That took guts,' he told himself, yet even as he did so it occurred to him that surely no woman could be worth such danger and inconvenience.

Cochise County Sheriff Johnny Behan really didn't like threatening the fairer sex, but he knew where his loyalties lay. The dapper lawman stood at the foot of Angie Sutter's bed and said his piece. He did his best to inject some menace into his delivery, but she was just too damned attractive. And if he'd known that a revolver muzzle was pointed directly at his midriff he would probably have struggled some more!

'So it would behove you to be on the Contention Stage tomorrow afternoon,' he concluded in what he hoped was a decisive manner.

Angie regarded him bleakly. 'Even though my wound might get to bleeding again?'

Behan sighed regretfully. He had expected that to be an issue. 'That's why it's the Contention Stage,' he responded patiently. 'It's the nearest town to Tombstone. You can rest up there for a while, before moving on. The county's paying the fare,' he added hopefully, 'and I'll even add a bit to cover your hotel for a few nights.'

'Very thoughtful of you,' she replied scathingly. 'But what if I don't want to move on without Rance?'

The sheriff coloured slightly. He really wasn't enjoying his role as messenger boy.

'Then we'll have to *put* you on the stage, in the interests of keeping the peace, you understand.'

Angie Sutter would dearly have loved to squeeze the trigger, but instead contented herself with a bold and robust response. 'When *Marshal* Toller gets back here, you sons of bitches won't know what peace is!'

CHAPTER NINE

Rance Toller stared long and hard at Horogan's blood-soaked body. He well knew that, but for a trick of fate it would have been his party shot to pieces and strewn about the surrounding landscape. Drew Williams's somewhat garbled tale had supplied the disconcerting reason for it, if not the real motive behind his own fortuitous presence there.

'You ever seen this fella before, Doc?'

'Can't say as I have,' Holliday responded pensively. His chest hurt and he was sweating heavily. 'Not that it matters a damn. He's just another hired gun. There's plenty of his kind around, only now it seems like some of them are after you.'

'All because I do my job properly,' Rance commented bitterly. 'And what of Angie? If I'm in danger, then so must she. God damn, but it makes my heart ache to think on it.'

His anguished train of thought was interrupted by an unwelcome tirade from Johnny Ringo. Of the three wounded prisoners, that man had stood up best to the arduous journey.

'Yo, Mr Wells Fargo man,' he taunted the very nervous recipient. 'Didn't figure you for a back-shooter! If you're not careful you'll get a taste for it. And say, wasn't it you who had me arrested back in Tombstone? All high and mighty then, wasn't you? Just like this poxy lawman and his lunger friend, only now you've got blood on your hands like the rest of us.'

Something snapped within Rance. Striding over to the sneering outlaw, he seized hold of his left leg and heaved him clean out of the saddle. Helplessly, Ringo flipped over onto his back and fell to earth … only to be painfully yanked up short by the handcuffs securing his right wrist to the saddle horn. As it was, his boots and then his knees slammed into the ground. A heavier man would have brought the horse down on top of him.

Even though seething with anger, the marshal had retained sufficient self-control to ensure that the impact did not strike Ringo's damaged shoulder. He fully intended that Angie's attacker should answer for his crime before a circuit judge, rather than bleed to death on the trail.

'Think on this, you miserable cockchafer,' Rance snarled. 'When we all return to Tombstone, anyone riding with me becomes a target and looking at you, I don't reckon you could survive many more gunshot wounds.'

With that, he left the winded and hurting outlaw to get back into the saddle unaided and returned to his deputy. Rance's heated words had pretty much highlighted their situation in a nutshell and they needed to make plans.

'Once Clanton runs his mouth off, they'll be watching for us coming,' he considered aloud. 'Yet that doesn't sit right. This man Gage isn't going to want a bloodbath in town. That would attract the sort of headlines he's trying to avoid.'

Holliday might have been physically ill, but there was nothing wrong with his thought processes. 'Which means he'll place the rest of his men south of town, ready to head us off and cover up any bloodletting.'

Rance nodded. 'So we need to swing wide and come in from the north.' Suddenly aware that Williams had joined them, he added, 'Are you with us or are you making your own way back?'

That man was sweating almost as much as Holliday, although for very different reasons. 'I've no choice. That oaf Clanton will have made me a marked man. Wells Fargo is a powerful business, but they couldn't protect me from an assassin's bullet and even if I was to survive an ambush they'd have nothing to go on.'

Holliday just couldn't resist. 'Bet you wish you'd stayed in Angie's hotel room, huh? *By her bedside.*'

Unwanted colour flooded in to Williams's cheeks, which didn't go unnoticed by Rance. His eyes were like gimlets as he put the question. 'Not that we're not grateful, you understand, but just what did bring you out here?'

The other man couldn't hide his discomfort. 'I told you, Angie feared for your life. She pleaded with me to follow that shootist. She even loaned me her Winchester, see?'

Rance nodded slowly. Something definitely didn't quite add up, but it would have been churlish to doubt the word of a man who had quite possibly saved their lives. 'Well then, you'd better hang on to it until you see her again.' Turning to his deputy, he added, 'It'll be dropping dark soon. Let's check on the prisoners and then head east for a ways. We'll cold camp for the night and move in on Tombstone at first light.'

Holliday was observing him intently, but suddenly his thin lips formed a wry smile. 'You know, on a new job it's really quite common for things not to go too well at first.'

Rance glanced at him sharply, but then he spotted the twinkle in his deputy's eye and the absurdity of the situation suddenly overwhelmed him. He laughed long and hard and felt all the better for it.

Holliday allowed the welcome mirth to run its course, but then couldn't avoid returning to harsh reality. 'However you look at it, we're likely to be a mite overmatched, Rance. You got any real idea how this is going to pan out?'

The marshal smiled grimly. 'Something'll come to me, Doc. It usually does.'

Darkness had fallen, but there was still work to be done in the offices of the Grand Central Mine. Superintendent E.B. Gage regarded the grubby figure before him with barely concealed distaste.

'So you mean to tell me that the local Wells Fargo agent shot one of *my* employees in the back. Why ever would he do something like that? It makes no sense. *Unless* it's just a pack of lies made up by you to extort money from me.' He glanced meaningfully over at the third man in the room, before returning his attention to the increasingly nervous informant.

Ike Clanton was beginning to wish that he'd just collected his wastrel brother from the Occidental Saloon and vamoosed. New Mexico Territory was barely two days' ride away, but provided the safety of a completely separate legal system. Trouble was, they needed a grubstake.

'Oh yeah, well, it makes sense if he's in league with that God damned marshal. Just think on it,' Ike replied belligerently, but then immediately regretted it. The sharp jab to his kidneys brought tears to his eyes and reminded him of just who he was dealing with. The hulking brute lurking in the shadows behind him was just one of many men employed by the mining superintendent.

'I meant no disrespect, Mr Gage,' he blurted out desperately. 'Only Williams might want Johnny Ringo behind bars as much as Toller does and just maybe he thought your man was going to spoil it all.'

'That was the intention,' the heavyset businessman replied dryly. 'I don't need all this frontier posturing. It's bad for business.'

Ike didn't know what the hell 'posturing' meant, but he sensed that Gage's mood was turning. 'Without me, you wouldn't know that Toller's still coming. That's got to be worth a few dollars.'

Gage favoured him with a chilling smile. Flickering light from the single kerosene lamp partially illuminated his smooth, well-fed features and somehow served to emphasize the latent menace in them. 'Yeah, well. I'll allow that knowledge could prove useful. So I'll tell you what. You just stick around until the marshal shows himself and maybe I'll cross your palm with silver. Lord knows there's enough of it in this burgh. How's that grab you? Ha ha ha.'

Without bothering to observe Clanton's disappointed reaction, he switched his attention to his enforcer. 'Captain Cullen, you will send your four *specialists* south of the town with orders to stop anyone approaching. There's something about this business that doesn't sit well, so round up some more men who can use a gun and keep them handy. The last thing I want is gunplay in town, but it's best to be prepared. Oh and take this … gentleman with you.'

The burly thug wore a store bought suit and bowler hat, all of which had completely failed to civilize his demeanour. Cullen's face bore the scars of numerous violent encounters, whilst his eyes possessed an unsettling quality that offered his victims no comfort whatsoever. He nodded silently, before slamming a meaty hand down onto Clanton's right shoulder and propelling him out of the office.

Gage suddenly recalled another matter. 'And have that woman's hotel watched,' he instructed, before waving them both away.

As the mining superintendent watched the two men depart he nodded thoughtfully. In less than one week, representatives of a big Chicago investor would be arriving to inspect the mining operation. He could not allow anything to spoil their favourable impression. The occasional Apache atrocity was totally beyond his control and therefore down to chance, but one way or another Marshal Toller would be history. Captain Cullen had never failed him before and of course there was always the woman over at the hotel. If necessary she would make a useful 'ace'.

Angie Sutter did not sleep well that night. Yet although her shoulder pained her, she refrained from drinking the laudanum at her bedside. Something told her that the revolver nestling by her right thigh was likely to see use before long and by imbibing opium and alcohol she might very possibly only succeed in blowing her own foot off. And so she passed the long hours of darkness dozing sporadically and fretting about Rance's possible whereabouts.

At one point, in that desperately lonely time before the dawn, Angie cried out his name. Unaccustomed fear gnawed at her guts and she began to weep into the pillow. Then her fierce determination and spirit began to reassert itself. Back in Dakota Territory, her husband had been gunned down before her very eyes. She had been left alone in the icy wastes to fend for herself and yet had managed to survive. Now she had found true happiness with another man and no one was going to take that away from her. Using the sheets to dab her tears, she drew in a deep breath and made a solemn vow. Whatever took place the following day, *nobody* would be manhandling her on to the Contention Stagecoach!

As the first rays of light appeared in the east, the six men were already mounted and on the move. The three prisoners had been resistant, so much so that one had incurred a livid bruise on his temple. Their destination was the north end of Tombstone and Rance was in no doubt that the day would bring much bloodshed.

'From what Drew says, I reckon I've already lost my job, but I sure ain't losing Angie as well,' he remarked quietly to Holliday.

His companion felt ghastly, but thus far the poor light had hidden that fact. 'I'm guessing that you've got some sort of plan,' he croaked, before hawking a stream of discoloured phlegm into the dirt.

Rance smiled grimly. He seemed to have been making a habit of that lately. 'I'm thinking that if Clanton did what he was threatening, then this man Gage will be expecting us. So we need a distraction. Are there any tunnels actually under the town or are they just in the hills around it?'

Holliday regarded him quizzically, his discomfort temporarily forgotten. His new friend definitely had him

100

intrigued. 'Oh sure,' he replied. 'Back in the seventies when Ed Schieffelin and his brother were prospecting around here, they dug everywhere. Those diggings are long played out now, but ...'

Rance couldn't stop himself. 'I'll bet all that I've got in my pockets that they didn't fill them in though, hey?'

Holliday furrowed his brow as he pondered just where this was leading. 'No ... no, they didn't.'

The marshal chuckled. 'So what I need now are some sticks of dynamite. Enough to make Gage think that his world's falling in.'

Doc Holliday burst out laughing, but then swiftly regretted it. When his inevitable and painful coughing fit finally subsided, he remarked in an exaggerated Southern drawl, 'It's no wonder you damn Yankees won the war. You just want to blow everything up!'

It was fully light by the time they had Tombstone's myriad buildings in sight. Rance reined in and dismounted. Motioning for Williams to join him, he got straight to the point. 'Whereabouts in town would I find some dynamite?'

The other man was plainly startled, but answered readily enough. 'There's a supply of it kept in a large shack at the rear of the Mining Exchange Building. It backs onto Safford Street at the north of town. You could just about make it out from here.'

'Any guards?' Rance demanded.

'Probably,' Williams replied. 'It costs a fortune to freight that stuff here.' He paused somewhat theatrically, before asking, 'You do realize it can be dangerous, don't you?'

'Hah,' Holliday responded, but the marshal merely

nodded and then moved swiftly on. 'Doc and I have got some things to take care of. We can't take these prisoners with us and after all that's happened I'm not turning them loose. Will you guard them for me until we make it back here?'

Drew Williams swallowed uncomfortably. Such a thing was actually the last thing that he wanted to do, but under Rance's intense scrutiny he could only nod his reluctant agreement.

'Law and order every time, that's what I say,' he remarked somewhat weakly, unaware that Holliday had drolly offered the same opinion a few days earlier.

'Good man,' the lawman earnestly responded and then turned to face Doc Holliday. It was the first time that day that he'd had a proper look at his deputy and what he saw chilled him to the bone. The consumptive displayed the pallor of a corpse and was trembling badly. 'You right sure you want to deal yourself into this, Doc? I *can* go it alone, you know.'

'Like hell you can,' Holliday brusquely replied. 'Anyhow, it's just the early morning shivers. I'll be fine once the sun heats up. Meantime, pass me that scatter-gun. Reckon that'll serve me better for the present.'

Rance regarded him dubiously, before reluctantly complying. Then he turned back to Williams. 'Care to lend me that buffalo gun? Where we're going, I could use the firepower.'

This time the Wells Fargo agent handed it over without comment. In truth it felt tainted with death and he was glad to be rid of it.

'I'll leave you with Angie's Winchester,' Rance added. 'Keep it trained on those bull turds and don't take any chances with them!' With that, he nodded to Holliday and the two men mounted up.

Williams watched uneasily as the marshal and his deputy rode slowly towards their town. He reflected, not for the first time in his life, that lust was a terrible thing. On this occasion it had mired him way out of his depth in something dark and dangerous. The only saving grace was that all his prisoners were wounded, with one likely to die from an infected leg.

Johnny Ringo saw matters somewhat differently. He had already decided that as soon as the two lawmen were out of sight he would be making a break for it. The fact that he was still handcuffed to the saddle horn just meant that he would be unable to take it easy on the Wells Fargo agent.

The single guard had obviously been on duty for a long time. He was tired, bored and completely oblivious of his surroundings. The large wooden shack constructed at the rear of the Mining Exchange Building faced out onto the relatively undeveloped Safford Street, the most northerly thoroughfare in Tombstone. Opposite lay only open ground, so there was little danger that Rance would be observed. With the horses ground-tethered some yards away, he simply moved in at speed. The sentry didn't detect his presence until it was too late. The marshal launched himself forward and brought the barrel of his Remington down on an unprotected skull with tremendous force. His victim collapsed without even a groan.

'You really are very good at that,' Holliday whispered admiringly.

'Years of practice,' Rance grunted as he frisked the man's

pockets. 'Damn and double damn. He hasn't even got the key to this place.'

The padlock was a massive brass heart-shaped affair. Shooting at it was out of the question, so Rance instructed, 'Keep a look out,' and raced back for his horse.

Soon he had a length of rope tied through the clasp, with the other end attached to his saddle horn. Spurring his horse forward, he was rewarded with a tremendous rending sound, as the whole obstruction was torn loose from its frame. Abruptly reining in, Rance left his mount tethered to the stricken door and cautiously entered the building. There before him lay a chest-high stack of small wooden crates with the legend *Du Pont Dynamite* inscribed on them.

Holliday had followed him in and now stared doubtfully at the high explosives. 'You ever use this stuff before?' he enquired.

'Once, up in the Dakotas,' Rance replied. 'It made quite an impression on me.' Glancing over at his scrawny deputy, he added, 'I reckon we can manage three crates between us and a coiled length of this fuse.' With that, he lifted one and placed it at Holliday's feet.

The voice at the entrance took them both by surprise. 'What the hell are you fellas about? Mr Gage will hear of this.'

Holliday swung around and levelled the sawn-off at the grimy newcomer. 'Maybe,' he allowed gruffly. 'But not from you. Now back up, so's I can take a look at you or by God I'll cut you in half!'

The startled miner stumbled backwards, colliding with the small group accompanying him. There were loud curses from those men unaware of the lethal danger before them.

'What in tarnation are you fellas doing here?' Holliday demanded. 'Answer me, or it'll go badly for you!'

The six men regarded him warily. All were unarmed except for belt knives and appeared to be in no itching hurry for trouble. Finally one of them replied, 'We've been sent for some cases of dynamite. We're blasting out a new tunnel, north of town.' Glancing nervously at the shotgun's gaping muzzles, he added, 'We don't want no hassle, mister.'

Rance appeared in the doorway and for the first time they noticed his badge of office. Before anyone could comment, he told them straight, 'My beef is with your boss, not you. But before you go about your business, we need your help. I want you to take us to the entrance of the nearest tunnel that stretches under the town.'

The group's spokesman eyed him curiously. 'You figuring on causing Gage some grief?'

Holliday cleared his throat noisily. 'Is that going to be a problem?'

The silver miners glanced at each other before breaking into broad grins. 'Hell, no,' one of them replied. 'It's time that fat robbing bastard felt some pain. Just don't blow up a whore house, OK?'

Despite the situation, Rance smiled his appreciation. 'It's a deal. You'd better get what you came for. Then we'll mix in, so's we just look like two more miners carrying explosives.'

All traces of humour disappeared as another of the group issued a terrifying warning. 'Just be careful with that stuff, Marshal. Some of it's been stored in there for a long time. Too long really. After a while the sticks start to sweat nitro-glycerine, which collects in the bottom of the box. Just

CHAPTER TEN

John Peters Ringo knew that he would never get a better chance to escape. The law dog and his 'lunger' friend were out of sight and Williams, left alone with three wounded outlaws, was already looking jumpy. Time to strike before the man's nerves got too strung out.

'Hey there, Mr Wells Fargo,' he called lightly. 'I've got me some chewing tobacco in my shirt pocket, but this arm's paining me something terrible. How's about helping out, huh?'

The other man regarded him with little sympathy. 'So use your right hand.'

Ringo shrugged regretfully and jiggled the handcuffs that secured his right wrist to the saddle horn. 'If only.'

Williams sighed impatiently. He was tempted to just ignore the lethal road agent and sometime rustler, but knew that he may well encounter him again at some point. It didn't make sense to deliberately antagonize him. 'OK, OK,' he said, reluctantly moving closer. He held Angie's Winchester tightly in both hands.

Without any warning, the heel of Ringo's left boot slammed squarely into his face, instantly breaking his nose. As an explosion of pain overwhelmed him, Williams tumbled down onto the unyielding ground. With that first massive strike, his fate was effectively sealed, because the still shackled outlaw couldn't afford to take any chances. Ringo slid out of the saddle and kicked his defenceless victim viciously in the ribs. As Williams instinctively tried to double up, he unwittingly brought his battered features closer and Ringo took full advantage. Again and again he kicked the Wells Fargo Agent's unprotected skull.

'For Christ's sake, that's enough, Johnny,' called out one of his companions, but he might as well have berated the wind.

Johnny Ringo, completely insensible to the throbbing pain in his left shoulder, was overwhelmed by a frenzied bloodlust, which didn't abate until Drew Williams had long since drawn his last breath. The dead man's skull was crushed to a nauseatingly slimy pulp that had both onlookers choking on their own bile.

Finally sated, Ringo closed his eyes for a long moment, before abruptly flicking them open to reveal the sickness that inhabited his mind. Without a word, he leapt up into the saddle. Seemingly oblivious to the sweat pouring from him, he suddenly recollected that he wasn't alone.

'I'm out of here,' he barked. 'You two sons of bitches can follow on if you choose, but remember … I've got the gun!' With that, he dug his heels in to his horse's flanks and took off to the northeast.

The two wounded rustlers glanced apprehensively over at Tombstone. They really didn't have any choice. The Wells Fargo agent had been a valued member of that community and its citizens would doubtless want revenge. Wearily, the two men urged their horses after their rapidly disappearing leader. Flies were already beginning to settle on the battered corpse and it now seemed very unlikely that Angie Sutter would ever get her rifle back!

With only one candle between them, the amount of light was limited, but it was sufficient to illuminate the tunnel face. What they saw gave them little comfort. The primitive diggings had been abandoned over two years earlier, once the silver bearing ore had been worked out. The timber side trees and roofing caps were mostly still in place, but there had been enough minor falls to make both men uneasy. Underground, they were well and truly out of their element and knew it. They were also unfamiliar with blasting techniques and more particularly the amount of dynamite to be used.

Rance had taken a chance with the six miners. After they had pointed out the tunnel entrance just west of the Chinese Quarter, he had allowed them to go about their business. They seemed to have no love for their employer and had even warned the two lawmen to beware of one particular man.

'Don't ever turn your back on Captain Cullen,' came the well-meant advice. 'In fact, try and avoid coming to any conclusions with him. He's one mean hombre!'

Crouched in their claustrophobic surroundings, the lawmen had other things to think on. With his badly weakened lungs, Holliday was slowly choking in the foul air and neither of them had any idea how much high explosive was required to penetrate the fourteen feet of earth above them.

'The hell with it,' croaked the desperate consumptive.

'Let's just use the lot and get out of this god damn tomb!'

Rance peered at him dubiously for some moments before reluctantly acquiescing. There was something else bothering him that he hadn't mentioned to his new friend. He didn't know exactly where the eruption would occur, except the fact that it would be somewhere in the northern part of town, on or around Fremont Street.

With the three crates pilled in a pyramid shape, he broke open the top one and gingerly removed a stick of dynamite. It was coated in a sticky substance that caused him to freeze in utter horror. 'Holy shit,' he whispered. 'It's sweating nitro!'

His immediate and foolhardy reaction was to wipe the stick clean. Only as globules of nitro collected on his fingers did he recognize his mistake … and what followed was an even bigger one. Instinctively he shook his hand to remove the substance and three minor explosions, like large firecrackers, occurred right next to the two men.

Holliday appeared to be on the point of collapse. 'By Christ,' he exclaimed. 'You're going to kill us both!' Desperately sucking in the foul air, he jabbed a bony finger at the high explosive. 'If it's got a blasting cap on it, just put it back in the box and fasten the extra length of fuse to it. That should give us time to get clear. I'm getting out of here before I pass out.' With that, he scrabbled to his feet and unsteadily began to make his way back up the tunnel.

'Oh great,' Rance muttered, knowing full well that the greatest risk now lay with him. Yet he really didn't have any choice. Very delicately he placed the unstable explosive back in the box and then tied the black match fuse onto its counterpart poking out of the stick of dynamite. Breathing a sigh of relief, he rubbed his gummy hand in the dirt and then retrieved a Lucifer from his pocket. As that flared into life, he swiftly backed off, uncoiling the fuse as he did so. Then came the moment of no return. He touched the burning stick to the black powder coated cotton string and quite simply fled.

Angie Sutter's eyes flicked open. The light of a new day, unimpeded by the unlined curtains, flooded into the room. She had slept heavily for an hour or two and felt drugged, but some inner voice urged her to get up ... quickly. After struggling out of bed, she moved purposefully over to the window. Sweeping the material aside with her right hand, the young woman peered out without really knowing what she was looking for. Despite the early hour, Allen Street had a fair amount of activity, with mineworkers heading out of town to join their shifts or walking to the various eating-houses. In all this bustle, the two idlers self-consciously loitering across the street stood out like a carbuncle. Scrutinizing *her* hotel appeared to be their only purpose.

The sudden noise was akin to muted thunder, except that instead of being up in the heavens it seemed to be down at street level. She had heard blasting from the diggings around Tombstone before, but this was definitely something different. A frightening tremor passed through the hotel that set the glass panes rattling directly in front of her. Nervously recoiling from the window, she nevertheless found her gaze drawn back to the two men.

In spite of, or possibly because of the violent occurrence, both of them were staring directly up at her room. Then, as a tremendous rending crash came from the northern part of town, they seemed to exchange heated words before one of them hurried off. The other one loosened the six-gun in his holster and then strode directly towards the entrance of the Grand Hotel. The moment that she had dreaded appeared to be upon her!

E.B. Gage, breakfasting in the Can Can Restaurant on 4th Street, knew exactly what the noise portended. Some moron had detonated a massive amount of dynamite within the town limits. The question was, why? Then he heard the sound of a wooden building collapsing and he thought he knew the reason. The Mining Exchange Building contained a huge safe, which held an eye-watering amount of cash belonging to the Grand Central Mine. More importantly to the heavy-set mining operative, it was also home to a vast amount of his own cash, illicitly obtained by manipulating contracts and other corrupt acts.

Glancing across at Captain Cullen's habitually silent figure, he snapped out, 'That sounded like the Exchange and you know what that means. Round up some men and get over there, fast!'

The massive enforcer could move very rapidly when he needed to. Slamming through the restaurant's door, he almost collided with his own man hotfooting it from the Grand Hotel. 'What the hell brings you here?' Cullen demanded.

That man's response demonstrated the honesty of a simpleton. 'I heard a noise!'

Rance had just raced across the threshold of the disused tunnel when the shockwave of the explosion caught him and quite literally lifted him off his feet. A blast of hot air washed over him as he lay in the dust, temporarily stunned. Coming to his senses, he became aware that at least one building was tearing itself apart.

'God damn fuses,' he muttered vaguely. It was obvious that he hadn't quite mastered the intricacies of blasting.

Skeletal fingers closed around his shoulders, as Holliday attempted to heave him to his feet. 'Your ma must have fed you well as a child,' that man grunted. 'I suggest we need to get out of here, while we can.'

Finally able to focus, Rance clambered to his feet. The sight that met his eyes was not what he had expected. At least a score of pigtailed Chinese milled around brandishing hand axes and meat cleavers. They were yelling unintelligible threats and obviously presumed that the *gwai lo*, or white devil, was attempting to destroy them all.

Holliday levelled his borrowed sawn-off at them and bellowed out, 'Stand off, you damned Celestials or it'll go badly for you!'

With his senses fully returned, Rance replied, 'The hell with them, let's make for the hotel. Hopefully all this chaos will have drawn off any guards.'

The premises of John Clum's *Epitaph* newspaper were barely three lots away from the epicentre of the manmade earthquake and it felt to him as though the world was coming to an end. As the floorboards shook violently beneath his feet, the prized barometer hanging on his office wall tumbled down and was irretrievably shattered. The sound of splintering timbers convinced him that the safest place to be was out in the open and so he raced into the front office, where his only employee was setting the typeface ready for the next edition. Together they rushed out onto Fremont Street and stared in awe at the trench that had opened up before them. There had been cave-ins before, but nothing quite like this. Even as they watched, the whole façade of the Mining Exchange Building, suddenly deprived of its underpinnings, fell forward onto the thoroughfare with a mighty crash.

Clum would have expected the vast cloud of choking dust to be a deterrent to any onlookers, but before long one man chose to ignore it. A big, burly fellow clutching a long barrelled Army Colt ploughed through it and carefully inspected the wreckage. The newspaper proprietor and town mayor would normally have joined him, but Captain Cullen's brooding presence always made him nervous. It was only when E.B. Gage and a number of other employees arrived that he made his way over to join them.

'Well?' demanded the mining superintendent anxiously. 'Have we been robbed or what?'

Cullen shook his massive head. 'Safe's sat there for all to see, Mr Gage, but the door's still closed.'

Before anyone else could speak, there was movement by the side of the wrecked building. Cullen swung his gun muzzle over, but then relaxed as he recognized the night watchman. The man staggered into view, holding his head.

'I don't understand any of this,' he announced mournfully. 'First somebody gives me hard knocks and then the god damned building falls down.' After emitting a deep sigh he added, 'I'm all played out,' and then slumped to his knees next to the deep channel.

E.B. Gage's piercing eyes settled on those of his chief

enforcer. 'What was this fool watching over?'

'The dynamite store.'

The mining boss blinked rapidly as his sharp mind put two and two together. 'Sweet Jesus, the hotel!' Swinging around, he glared at the startled mayor. 'Dime to a dollar, this is your new lawman's doing. He's pulled us off to rescue his bitch!'

Angie Sutter had returned to her sick bed. In her right hand, concealed by a fold in the sheet, she held Drew Williams's Colt revolver. It was cocked and aimed at the only door. She didn't have long to wait. Heavy footsteps sounded on the landing and then the door burst open without any warning. The weasel-faced individual that she had seen down on the street stepped across the threshold, right hand caressing his gun butt. Confronted by an attractive young woman, reclining in bed with her left shoulder heavily bandaged, he was temporarily stumped.

'You might have knocked,' she stated calmly.

The intruder stared at her askance for a long moment before finally recovering some of his limited wits. 'I'm here under orders,' he responded brusquely, as though that excused everything.

At that instant, more footsteps rang out, this time on the stairs and the man drew his revolver. Swiftly he moved around behind the open door and waited to see who appeared.

The two men pounded up the stairway, Rance in the lead and Holliday struggling on some distance behind. As the marshal reached the top, he unexpectedly found himself able to peer straight into Angie's bedroom. His face lit up with sheer delight at the sight of her and yet strangely she did not reciprocate. Her features were grim and strained and then suddenly he saw the gun in her hand, apparently pointing in his general direction.

'Sweet Jesus, Angie. It's me,' he cried out desperately and then she fired.

In the confines of the room, the noise was deafening. A cloud of smoke obstructed Angie's view, but an agonized scream confirmed that her aim had been true. With a loud thump, the hidden gunman collapsed onto the floor. Blood coated his jacket as he twitched uncontrollably. By the time Rance gingerly stepped through the doorway, there was only a corpse awaiting him. Although desperate to hold his lover, the lawman maintained his professional manner for just a little longer.

'He alone?'

Angie nodded. 'For the moment. He had a sidekick in the street who ran off when that earthquake happened. Or whatever it was.' She looked at him strangely. 'That wasn't something to do with you, was it?'

Rance could contain his joy and relief no longer. Rushing over to the bed, he took her tenderly in his arms and smothered her in kisses. She responded eagerly and for a few moments they were completely oblivious to everything but each other.

Doc Holliday finally arrived in the room, wheezing badly. 'Huh, it's all right for some,' he gasped. 'I don't even get a howdy-do.'

Angie prised herself free from Rance's grasp. 'Well, hello there, Doc,' she responded with a chuckle. Still clutching the handgun, she eased out of bed and padded over to him. 'As you can see, your patient is on the mend. You did good. Real good.' With that, she unthinkingly leaned forward with the intention of planting an affectionate kiss on his lips.

Instinctively he turned away, so that it instead landed on his cheek. He was all too aware that consumption was contagious. 'I wouldn't wish this on you,' he muttered, smiling as he saw the sudden realization in her eyes. Then, glancing down at the bloody cadaver he enquired, 'What did that sack of shit want, anyhow?'

It was Tombstone's Marshal over by the window who answered that. 'The same as these fellas, I guess.'

CHAPTER ELEVEN

For once in his life E.B. Gage was flummoxed. The lawman that he so badly wanted rid of, had miraculously managed to return to his own jurisdiction. The question was, just how badly did the marshal want to stick around? Could he be bought off or was he one of those thankfully rare individuals who just wouldn't bend? It made most sense to get rid of him quietly, by negotiation and yet ... the superintendent possessed a malicious streak that took exception to this man Toller partially destroying one of Tombstone's most important buildings.

'Captain Cullen. Get into that hotel and find out what our marshal intends doing next. See what you make of the man. No violence mind ... just yet. You will find me in Hafford's when you're done. Oh and it would be worth getting your four professionals back into town. We might have need of them.'

As the enforcer moved off to do his bidding, Gage fixed his hard eyes on John Clum. '*Whatever* happens today, if any of it gets written up in the *Epitaph* it'll be your epitaph. Savvy?'

The newspaper editor blanched. As a former Indian

agent at the San Carlos Reservation, he had resigned in protest at the treatment of the Apaches there and loathed being browbeaten by people in positions of power. This time, however, he had a good retort. 'Fair enough, Mr Gage, but I can't answer for those folks over at the *Nugget*. They're a mite independent in their reporting.'

He was rewarded by a sigh of petulant annoyance from the other man, before moving away to await further developments in peace. They would not be long in coming.

Cullen didn't like the look of this Marshal Toller. He wore his badge of office for all to see and appeared reasonable enough, but there was something about him. It was the eyes that gave him away. They were the eyes of a killer and Captain Cullen knew all about such things. Then he saw the 1876 Winchester in Toller's hands and knew that there could be only one outcome to all of this.

'Nice rifle. You had it long?'

'It's on loan,' Rance responded coldly. 'But the original owner is past caring about such things.'

The two men were facing each other on the stairs of the Grand Hotel. Rance had the tactical advantage because he was at the top and pointing a long gun, but none of that really mattered. There wouldn't be any shooting … just yet.

Cullen's mouth was set like a trap. Horogan had been a very good man, in that he did as he was told and killed with ruthless efficiency. Such useful individuals were surprisingly hard to find. Yet to E.B. Gage they were just mere pawns in the never ceasing quest for wealth and the captain abruptly recollected that he had a job to do.

'So what has to happen to end this peacefully?'

Rance regarded the big man implacably. He knew exactly what his terms were. 'I've got some prisoners waiting outside of town. They'll need doctoring and then locking up until the circuit judge arrives. He'll probably dismiss the rustling charges because they happened outside my jurisdiction, but I want Johnny Ringo on trial for the attempted murder of Angie Sutter right here in Tombstone. By then she will have recovered enough for us to ride out of here. So if the citizens committee wants my badge, they're welcome to it ... then.'

Cullen regarded the lawman with grudging admiration. 'You caught up with Ringo, huh? I'd happily settle that snake for you. Why don't I stake him out in the desert and work on him with Mesquite thorns? That's got to be better than anything a judge can hand out. And that way you can hit the trail now, with everyone happy.'

Rance favoured him with a cold smile. 'I'll allow that he deserves it, but he'll answer to the law.'

'And what about that damned building you blew up?' the enforcer snapped. 'That wasn't very lawful, was it?'

'Who's to say it wasn't an act of God? Besides, I had good reason to feel that I feared for my life ... and nothing's changed.' The lawman was beginning to tire of the exchange. 'Now go back to your boss and tell him how it's got to be.'

'Just like that,' Cullen scoffed. 'You really don't know what you're up against, do you?'

'I don't give a damn,' Rance retorted angrily. 'What I do know is that ...'

What he was about to say was lost in the abrupt din of shattering glass and splintering timber. Angie's bedroom was under fire and all bets were off.

*

120

The two surviving Clanton brothers had been drinking all through the night, but whereas Phin became mellow and affable in his cups, Ike's natural belligerence only seemed to increase. The more cheap whiskey he drank, the more aggrieved he felt over the hand that life had dealt him and in particular the persecution he had suffered from Marshal Rance Toller.

'That son of a bitch burned my god damned house down,' he ranted at anyone who would listen. 'Even Wyatt Earp didn't go that far!'

Come daybreak, with his nose like a beetroot and eyes blood red, his sense of injustice had reached a climax and he finally decided to do something about it. All he had to hand was a Colt revolver, so that would have to do. Even severely drunk, he shied away from a face-to-face confrontation. That had never been his way. Far better to shoot from concealment.

Unnoticed by the Occidental's hardened drinkers, Ike slowly made his way upstairs. He found an open front window directly facing onto the Grand Hotel and one of Cullen's men had already let slip which window belonged to the marshal's woman. Laboriously, he checked the loads in his gun and so obsessed was he that he barely even noticed the muffled explosion or even the destruction that followed on. What he did spot was Toller and Holliday hurriedly entering the hotel. Ike still harboured a grudge against the 'lunger' for his involvement in brother Billy's death, so any indiscriminate shooting was now doubly justified.

The sound of a gunshot in the hotel perplexed his addled mind, but didn't distract him from his deadly purpose. He could make out movement in the room through the open curtains and decided that the time had come. After tortuously cocking the hammer, he rested his arm on the window ledge and vainly attempted to stop the muzzle wavering. So intense was his concentration that he didn't notice Captain Cullen's arrival.

With rivulets of sweat pouring down his face, Ike finally gave up on any pretence at accuracy. 'The hell with it,' he announced and squeezed the trigger. As the first bullet sped into the Grand Hotel, he felt a surge of exhilaration and just kept on firing.

'You treacherous bastard,' Rance snarled as he swung his rifle muzzle towards Gage's chief enforcer.

That man appeared genuinely shocked, but nevertheless reacted with practised speed. Drawing his revolver, Cullen dropped back down the stairs just in time. As the powerful Winchester fired, he felt the blast of pressure above his head from the near miss. Recognizing that he was outgunned, the big man hurriedly retreated through the hotel lobby. As the solitary desk clerk wisely dropped down below the level of the counter, Cullen bellowed back towards the stairs.

'Believe me, Marshal, that was none of my doing.'

Any response was lost in the massive detonation in the room above, as Doc Holliday unleashed both barrels of his sawn-off through the shattered window. Knowing that any chance for further negotiation was gone, Captain Cullen turned on his heels and after making sure that his men across the street knew who it was, he cautiously left the hotel.

Holliday replaced the two twelve-gauge cartridges and slammed the breech shut. The room was full of acrid smoke and he was deaf in his right ear.

'Seems like Tombstone's going to be living up to its name again,' he muttered as he backed away from the window. Then his eyes met Rance's, as that individual rushed anxiously into the room and he smiled reassuringly. Both he and Angie had been untouched by the burst of shooting across the thoroughfare.

'This is a real friendly town we've fetched up in,' the marshal remarked sarcastically, entirely failing to hide his relief at her survival. 'It looks as though we've got a fight on our hands, Doc. And that's the last thing I wanted.'

The other man seemed less concerned. After all, as he kept reminding everyone, he was dying anyway. 'Well, if that's the case, we'd better sort out our dispositions,' he drawled remarkably calmly. 'I always wanted the whole floor of a hotel to myself. Now's the time to try it.'

Rance caught on immediately. 'Can you keep an eye on the street for us?' he asked Angie. 'We need to evict the other guests.'

So saying, he led his deputy out onto the landing and began hammering on doors. There were a surprising number of people in the other bedrooms. Salesmen, card-sharps, prospectors living high on the back of a minor silver strike and even a couple of prostitutes. Gunfire was not unusual in Tombstone and so none of them had thought to investigate the shooting. It took harsh words and threats of violence to get them all out, but finally Rance and his two companions had the upper floor of the Grand Hotel to themselves.

'Lock all the doors and leave the keys in the locks,' the lawman instructed. Moving back into Angie's room, he seized the fresh corpse by its boots and dragged it over to the top of the stairs. 'Hopefully we'll be out of here before this fella starts to turn,' he commented optimistically.

'Rance,' Angie called out. 'There's some movement in the street. Looks like Sheriff Behan has arrived.'

'Huzzah!' yelled Holliday mockingly. 'We can all sleep safe in our beds tonight.'

As Captain Cullen approached Hafford's Saloon, the last thing he would have expected to see was Mr E.B. Gage holding his head in his hands. Then he noticed the blood and he realized that something pretty damned serious had occurred.

Several small pieces of shot from Holliday's twelve-gauge cartridges had badly lacerated the mining superintendent's face and one had torn away a chunk of his right ear. The wounds were apparently sufficiently painful and disfiguring as to almost guarantee extreme retribution. As though recognizing his chief enforcer's footfall, Gage raised his head and fixed a pair of feverish eyes on him. Although obviously suffering from shock, he clearly had sufficient control to issue some very uncompromising orders.

'I don't know who started the shooting, but I'm going to finish it,' he snarled. Bloodstained spittle flew from his lips as he continued. 'I'm not interested in what you discussed with that god damned marshal. He's crossed a line and I just want him dead, along with anyone who stands with him. Do whatever it takes, just get him. Understand?'

Cullen nodded silently. Contrary to general perception, he did not actually enjoy killing people, but he was very skilled at it. He would get the marshal, but he had one suggestion to make and was prepared to stand his ground. 'Mr Gage, killing the woman is a sure way to get a mention in the newspapers. I would recommend against it.'

Gage stared at him mutely for a moment. He knew that the captain could not easily be browbeaten and in any case he suddenly didn't care. Sheriff Behan had appeared before them and made an easier target.

'Do what you wish, captain,' he answered dismissively, before savagely turning on the county lawman. 'What the hell do you want, you weasel-faced shit? There's enough law around here already.'

Johnny Behan appeared both surprised and hurt. He fingered the angry gash in his scalp as he replied. 'I have no jurisdiction in town and I certainly haven't come to meddle. I just have a personal interest in seeing what befalls Marshal Toller.'

Gage grunted his understanding and moderated his tone. Wincing with the pain of his wounds he said, 'Then we both have a vested interest in seeing how well Captain Cullen performs.' Turning away, he bellowed out, 'Where the hell's that sawbones? This isn't bordello rouge, you know. It's *my* blood!'

It was at that moment that the dislodged guests spilled out onto the dusty street, thereby giving Gage's men the opportunity they needed. For the first time since the highly embellished shootout at the O.K. Corral, there was going to be real terror in Tombstone.

Some sixth sense alerted Rance to what was about to happen. 'Let's get that mattress off the bed and into the corner.' He knew full well that although it wouldn't stop a bullet, it could protect them from splinters. They were only just in time.

As the three of them hunkered down behind it, a fusillade

of shots rang out and suddenly the air was alive with flying lead. Because of the angle from the street, the bullets all went high, but it felt as though the room was disintegrating around them. Fragments of wood and glass struck their barricade and as the gunfire relentlessly continued it was obvious that their attackers had no shortage of ammunition.

'I'm sorry I got the both of you into this,' Rance yelled over the din. Before either of his companions could reply, he added, 'They ain't just taking pot-shots for the fun of it. It's to keep our heads down while they make their move. If we stay like this, we're finished!'

Doc Holliday wasn't new to gunplay, but he didn't have Rance's long experience as a lawman. 'So how do you figure it?' he demanded.

'We need to hold that landing. They'll either attack up the stairs or come through a back window … or both. Are you with me?'

Holliday was vaguely insulted. 'That's a hell of a thing to ask.'

As the two men scrambled clear of the mattress, Rance swung around to face Angie. His features were an unsettling blend of ferocity and tenderness. 'You've already taken one bullet in this town. If you love me, you'll stay put. Savvy?'

Before she had the chance to answer, Holliday called out, 'There's movement in the lobby,' and Rance was gone.

The four gunmen were confident that the rate of fire from outside would keep their prey pinned down in the bedroom. And there was something else as well. They knew about the other part of Cullen's plan.

All clutching revolvers for rapid firing at close range, they moved up to the half landing. At this point the stairway took a ninety-degree turn to the left. With bullets continuing to ricochet in the front bedroom, all seemed to be going well. Then they saw the bloodied corpse blocking the head of the stairs and they hesitated. It was decision time, but Doc Holliday didn't give them the opportunity.

With abject horror, Cullen's thugs watched the gaping muzzles of a twelve gauge sawn-off slide over the top of the cadaver and then all hell broke loose. With a tremendous crash, the big gun belched its deadly load. Two of the men died instantly, bloodily torn to pieces by the spread of shot, whilst a third lost the little finger of his left hand. While Holliday reloaded, Rance fired his 45-70 Winchester at the fourth man and literally blew him back into the lobby.

Dripping blood from his painful wound, the sole survivor fled. Levering in another cartridge, Rance called down to his companion, 'We've got the high ground, Doc. Let's see if we can keep it. I'm going to check the bedrooms.'

With that, he moved off down the corridor to listen at each of the doors. At the far end, where the room faced out over an alleyway leading onto Tough Nut Street, the marshal heard the sound of a boot dragging on the window ledge. It was enough to send him scurrying back to Angie's bedroom.

'Come with me,' he demanded brusquely.

Despite the parlous situation, she peered up at him mischievously. 'I love you, so I'm staying here,' she announced.

Rance stared at her incredulously. 'For Christ's sake. This is no time for …' Shutting his mouth like a trap, he reached into his jacket and produced a stick of dynamite. 'I can't do it all myself,' he explained impatiently. 'I need your help.'

Eyes widening in horror at the sight of the high explosive,

Angie responded with, 'Oh, not again,' but nevertheless she awkwardly got to her feet and followed him back down the corridor.

Back outside the end room, Rance listened carefully. He heard more movement and whispered voices and decided that there were probably a fair few gun hands gathered in there. There was no time to lose. Placing his rifle on the floor, he retrieved and lit a Lucifer.

'Unlock the door and then run like hell,' he hissed.

Even as her right hand grasped the key, he placed the naked flame to the end of the short fuse. As it flared into vivid life, Angie twisted her wrist sharply and then backed off fast. Rance eased the door ajar and tossed the lethal baton into the room. Knowing full well what their reaction would be, he darted to the side and closed the door. As the key turned in the lock, gunfire crashed out and numerous bullets splintered the woodwork.

Grabbing his Winchester, he raced back down the corridor and bellowed out, 'Fire in the hole, Doc!'

The words were barely out of his mouth when there was a tremendous explosion at the rear of the hotel. The whole building shook and the door that he had just locked blew out into the hallway. As dust showered down from the timbered ceiling, Rance ground to a halt and then cautiously retraced his steps. The lack of any screaming indicated that he would find no survivors and so it proved. Four men, their bodies charred and bloody, were dimly visible, sprawled about in the blackened room.

With some of the floorboards buckled, the lawman tentatively advanced through the smoke filled slaughterhouse like an avenging wraith. Reaching the window, he unsurprisingly found that all the glass had been blown out into the alley below. Glancing out, he saw a solitary gunman staring up at the devastated hotel room in stunned disbelief.

Favouring that individual with a grim smile, Rance snapped the Winchester up to his shoulder and swiftly took aim. He was wasting his time, because the sole survivor of the assault party took off as though the hounds of hell were at his heels.

'Tell them what you saw,' his tormenter hollered after him, before turning away from the empty window. Rance felt pretty damn certain that Gage's men wouldn't try that again, but he also knew that it wasn't over yet.

CHAPTER TWELVE

'This buffalo gun needs to be outside,' Rance announced, brandishing his powerful Winchester. 'I'm going up on the roof. Angie, stay with Doc ... *please.*'

The gunfire from opposite the front of the hotel had slackened off to the occasional optimistic pot shot. It was as though their besiegers had sensed that things hadn't gone well.

With the aid of a chair, the marshal clambered through a trapdoor in the ceiling and was soon crawling over to the wooden façade fronting onto Allen Street. Across and to the right of his position was the Occidental Saloon and as he cautiously glanced over the top, Rance's gaze took in a sight that made his blood boil. Ike Clanton, having fired his six, had collapsed on the window ledge in a drunken stupor, still clutching his empty revolver. Suddenly everything became very clear.

'Son of a bitch!' Rance snarled as he quickly sighted down the twenty-four inch barrel and snapped off a shot. At such close range it should have been a certainty, but his accuracy was influenced by anger and so the bullet merely slammed into the window frame next to Ike's head. A vicious splinter the shape of a cactus spine, but much thicker lanced into the rustler's cheek and with a howl of pain he jerked awake. With blood streaming down his chin and completely oblivious to the cause of his sudden distress, he instinctively pulled away from the window and stumbled for the stairs.

Rance cursed vividly and switched his attention off to his left, to the group of men congregated near Hafford's Saloon. Confused by the apparently random shot, they were backing off towards the interior. 'Who's in charge down there?' he bellowed.

'I am,' came the rapid response, instantly followed by another voice from inside.

'Like hell he is. I am!'

'Huh, too many chiefs,' the marshal muttered to himself, before trying again. 'You know, it doesn't have to be like this. All I want is to do my job and then ride out.'

A more imaginative individual might have recognized the incongruity of a man swearing to uphold the law and then laying waste to his own town, but Rance Toller only ever saw what was directly before him and right now that meant just one thing: hauling Johnny Ringo before a judge!

A gruff voice that he remembered from his negotiations in the hotel replied, 'You know how many dead we got?'

'Probably more than you realize,' Rance dryly said. 'And there'll likely be plenty more if you don't see sense.'

The only response to that was a volley of shots. As wood chips erupted from the ornate façade, the frustrated lawman backed off and drew out the second of the three sticks of dynamite that he had stashed in his jacket. Using another of his precious Lucifers, he got the fuse burning and then leapt forward. Gauging the distance, Rance lobbed the hissing projectile towards Hafford's. Even as he did so, something blazing hot scored the side of his head and caused him to drop to his knees in shock.

Across the street, there was a tremendous detonation as the dynamite exploded in the doorway of the saloon. All the windows blew in and one of Cullen's men began a long, penetrating scream that hung in the air until every man present prayed for it to cease. Rance had intended to follow up with sustained rifle fire, but he had lost his chance. Blood trickled down his face from the glancing bullet wound and he felt shaky and nauseous. Lady luck had definitely been with him, but he did just wonder how long she would linger.

E.B. Gage was experiencing a rare bout of incandescent rage, which had completely inundated his normally calm and objective demeanour. His already painful wounds were now singed and blackened. The flatteringly cut, expensive suit hung about his portly figure in rags and the continuous screaming was shredding his overstretched nerves.

'For Christ's sake, put that man out of *our* misery,' he bawled over at Captain Cullen. 'And then get over here.'

The tormented hired gun was quite obviously beyond the medical ability of any frontier doctor and so mere seconds passed before another gunshot rang out. When Cullen appeared before his employer, his habitually poker-faced expression was gone, replaced by an air of sullen resentment.

'There's too much blood being spent, Mr Gage,' he announced wearily. 'Maybe we should just let this man Toller do what he needs to and then send him on his way. Him bringing Ringo before a judge ain't gonna upset your plans any.'

Gage gave a very fair impression of someone afflicted with rabies. As he answered his chief enforcer, he was practically foaming at the mouth. 'I don't give a shit about his needs or even *my* plans anymore. Nobody rides roughshod over Elijah Benton Gage.' He paused momentarily to draw breath and collect his thoughts. 'Just supposing that he's actually left us with some of *our* dynamite, I want you to get some from the store. Enough to raise that hotel to the ground ... and everyone in it!'

Cullen was horrified. 'This doesn't sit well with me, Mr Gage. I'm a problem solver, but I didn't sign on for open warfare. Besides, there's a female in there and a right pretty one by all accounts.'

Gage glowered balefully at him. 'I'm not interested in some fast trick. I've given you an order, God damn it and I expect it to be obeyed.'

The other man stared at him long and hard before finally acquiescing, but it came with a condition. 'Yeah, well, if this all goes wrong, don't ever give me another!'

Rance Toller still wasn't quite himself, but he had enough sense to call below. 'Hold your fire, Doc. I'm coming down.'

Holliday still held the stairs, but he looked grim. Beads of sweat coated his face and his latest handkerchief was spattered with fresh blood. Angie was stationed by the ruined window and when she saw him came hurrying over, her anxiety was plain to see.

'God almighty, Rance. You're hit!'

Her deep concern warmed his heart, but he was quick to dismiss its cause. 'It's just a scratch, although I'll allow it nearly finished me. What's happening out on the street?'

She began to dab at the blood on his cheek, but knew better than not to answer. 'It's deserted. There's not a soul about. Even the drunks in the Occidental are keeping quiet.'

Very gently, he pushed her hand away from his face, but kept an affectionate hold on it as he walked with her into the devastated bedroom. Carefully peering outside, Rance saw the makings of a 'ghost town', but it gave him no comfort whatsoever. It was just *too* quiet. Stepping back, he gazed at Angie's lovely but troubled features. His biggest regret was that he had involved her in such a bloody nightmare, but it was no time for self-recriminations. The beleaguered lawman came to a decision and as usual with him, it had to be acted on immediately.

'Doc, we're getting out of here. Right now. Is there anyone down in the lobby?'

'Only dead bodies.'

And so it proved. As the three of them cautiously made their way through the hotel, they didn't encounter a living soul.

Holliday choked down yet another cough, before growling, 'Just what's on your mind, Rance? Why are we abandoning such a defensible position?'

Pausing in the gloomy rear passage, the marshal whispered, 'If it was me out there, I'd be looking to repay in kind. They've got enough explosives left to level the town and I reckon we've got under their skins a mite.'

Holliday stared at him with wide-eyed astonishment. 'You and I should have hooked up sooner. You really have got a dark turn of mind for a peace officer.'

The dwindling group of gunmen regarded Captain Cullen

dubiously as he packed the sticks of dynamite into a well-worn carpetbag. They were used to handling all kinds of firearms, but high explosives were a different matter. Their discomfort was heightened by the glowering presence of their employer at the rear of Hafford's Saloon.

E.B. Gage winced with pain as the town's doctor smeared some form of disgusting looking substance onto his burns. The fact that it looked like axle grease and quite probably was, did nothing to improve his foul humour.

'Who are you going to get to deliver that package?' he barked down the room.

Cullen regarded him sourly. 'I wouldn't tell my men to do anything that I was afraid to do, so it'll be me.'

Gage was too consumed with a desire for vengeance to concern himself with such niceties. 'Huh, very noble, I'm sure. Just make sure you do it right.'

Without sparing his boss a second glance, Cullen ensured that the single fuse was properly wedged in a blasting cap before nodding at the man who was to accompany him. Together they advanced to the saloon's ruined frontage. His other four enforcers followed on and took up positions nearby.

'Remember,' he instructed, 'don't fire unless we're fired at. And when this goes in, hit the deck.' Drawing in a deep breath, he glanced at his companion. 'You'd better have those Lucifers ready, because I don't aim to hang around out there.'

Cullen well knew that this was the most dangerous part. Anybody waiting in the upper floor of the Grand would have little trouble picking him off, but then that was what he drew his pay for.

'The hell with it,' he snapped. 'Let's go!'

The two men burst from cover and moved diagonally across Allen Street. They fully expected to be met by a hail of lead, but all remained quiet. If Cullen hadn't had more pressing matters on his mind, he might have considered that odd. As it was, he was just glad to be still alive.

Stopping directly below Angie's bedroom, he nodded at his assistant and a Lucifer flared into life. Seconds later, the seemingly innocent carpetbag was hurled with tremendous effort, hissing and spitting, into the doomed hotel. Without another glance, the two men raced back across the street. Nobody really knew what would happen next.

The three fugitives tentatively stepped out into the alleyway at the rear of the hotel. Other buildings backed onto the alley and directly facing them was a small corral belonging to the Pioneer Livery. Both men had their weapons cocked and ready, but there didn't seem to be any sign of opposition. In fact, there was nobody at all in sight. The explosions and unusual amount of gunfire seemed to have resulted in all the townsfolk sheltering indoors.

'Let's get to the livery and see if anything happens,' instructed Rance prophetically.

Watching intently for any sign of movement, they walked steadily over to the corral. A number of horses were enclosed, but they showed little interest in the approaching humans. With an ear-splitting roar, an entire wing of the Grand Hotel abruptly disintegrated in a storm of shattered timber. The blast of pressure from the explosion sent all three of them tumbling to the ground and it was that that saved them from gruesome injury. Jagged splinters swept over their heads and on into the livery, creating bloody havoc amongst the animals. Angie cried out in pain, but it was merely due to the hard landing jarring her left shoulder.

As at the Mining Exchange Building, a huge cloud of dust seemed to hang in the air before gradually drifting to earth. Twisting around, Rance gazed at the stunning devastation. Unlike his companions, he felt little sense of surprise. He had expected some such action and the savagery of it only served to fuel the burning rage within. The fact that Tombstone's serving lawman had only recently carried out a similar indiscriminate attack was completely lost on him. Gage's men had quite obviously targeted Angie's bedroom and that was more than enough to justify any retribution that followed.

'Come on, Doc,' he snarled, clambering to his feet. 'Let's give them hell while they least expect it.'

Holliday slowly struggled to join him, but then began choking on the settling dust and fell back to the ground.

Impatiently, Rance grabbed him under both armpits and heaved. 'This ain't no time for laying around,' he observed dryly. Then he glanced down at Angie and his expression softened. 'You stay right where you are … *please.*' It briefly occurred to him that she had actually obeyed him recently. 'I don't want you anywhere near us until we've set things aright.'

Still shaken by her fall, she nodded silently and doing so freed her two companions to pursue their own agenda.

The two men regarded each other appraisingly. Rance saw a stick thin consumptive in a dust-covered frockcoat, who had inexplicably stuck with him through very trying times. The former dentist was obviously very weak, but the fierce gleam in his eyes confirmed what Rance had already surmised. Doc Holliday actually enjoyed killing. It appeared that it was the only time when he felt truly alive. In turn, the Southerner recognized that the so-called peace officer was actually a very dangerous man, masquerading behind a tin badge. Sure, he was loyal to his friends and he did have a certain code of behaviour known as 'the rules' that he paid lip service to, but underneath it all, Marshal Toller was a born killer of men.

'So what's the plan, *Marshal?*' Holliday croaked breathlessly. 'You always seem to have one.'

'I've heard that said and yes, I do happen to have one. We go through what's left of the hotel and straight down their throats while they least expect it.'

'That's a plan?' queried Holliday incredulously.

Rance patted a scrawny shoulder. 'It's the best one you'll hear today. Now let's move. We're burning daylight!'

Without a backward glance, the two men moved off towards the smoking devastation that was the Grand Hotel. They were accompanied by the agonized whinnying of horribly wounded horses in the Pioneer's Corral, but sadly they would have to keep, lest all surprise was lost.

The marshal and his deputy prowled carefully through the wreckage. Their three victims on the stairs had disappeared under a pile of misshapen timber and Angie's bedroom simply no longer existed. Amazingly the hotel entrance still stood, but everything to the right of it had collapsed.

Rance nodded. 'When we go through those doors, shoot anyone holding a gun.' He paused momentarily. 'Oh and thanks, Doc!'

The other man merely offered a thin smile. Holliday's

deadly sawn-off had both hammers cocked. His feverish stare and drooping black moustache seemed to imbue him with a demonic quality. He was ready. Rance clutched Horogan's Winchester in his left hand, whilst in his right he held his well-worn Remington. He well knew that a revolver was more suited to a short-range melee and he too was ready. Side by side they approached the threshold.

Captain Cullen simply couldn't believe the destruction that he had wrought. He didn't know the hotel owner personally and it was probably just as well.

'Get over there, Cullen, and search for bodies,' Gage demanded. 'You find anything, be sure and tell the undertaker. Ha ha ha.' The pain from his wounds was still intolerable, but already he was beginning to feel a bit better.

His enforcer regarded him bleakly. Cullen felt almost physically sick at what his handiwork had likely done to the pretty little lady. It exceeded anything that he had done in his chequered army career. He could think of many things to say, all of them obscene and he only just kept a rein on his temper. Nodding grimly to his five remaining able bodied men; he strode back through the battered saloon towards the street. All of them had their weapons drawn, but none of them expected to need them. The dynamite had served their employer only too well.

As the six gun thugs moved reluctantly towards the ruined structure, something totally unforeseen occurred. Two supposedly dead men abruptly swept through the entrance like avenging spectres and opened fire at almost point blank range. In their ignorance of the true situation, Gage's enforcers had approached in an ill-advised cluster and it was about to cost them dear.

Doc Holliday discharged both barrels in rapid succession and even amongst hardened professionals, the effect was shocking. Two men each caught a full load in their chest, but stray pieces of shot also lacerated some of their cronies. Recognizing their most dangerous adversary, Rance fired his revolver at Cullen. He had aimed dead centre, but that individual had reacted faster than his men and was already on the move. The heavy bullet struck him left of centre, breaking a rib and then punching out a nasty exit wound.

Holliday hurled the smoking scatter-gun at those still standing and then calmly drew his revolver. This was his second shootout on the dusty streets of Tombstone. He had no particular desire to survive it, but he intended to ensure that none of his opponents did either. Rapidly drawing a bead on the nearest man, he fired. His victim received a mortal wound in the throat and, choking on his own blood, staggered away from his comrades.

Rance momentarily ignored the wounded Cullen and aimed at those still unhurt. One of them had to ward off the heavy shotgun and so the lawman swept on and fired into the face of the next. That unfortunate was sporting a natty bowler hat and as the horrific injury snapped his head back, the 'city slicker' headgear incongruously rolled off along Allen Street.

Even though in great pain and struggling to stay on his feet, Cullen could see that his fellow enforcers were falling around him. Two men appeared to be overwhelming six and his professional pride simply could not accept it. Desperately straining to concentrate, he snapped off a shot at the black clad cardsharp who had just succeeded in killing his third victim. The bullet ploughed a bloody furrow in Holliday's right thigh and sent him spiralling to the ground.

Out of his peripheral vision, Rance saw his companion fall.

'Doc!' he called out in alarm and then turned his malevolent attention onto the wounded enforcer.

Driven by murderous rage, he unwisely emptied his remaining chambers into Cullen's bulky torso. That man's body jerked violently under the repeated impacts and then lay perfectly still, his jacket literally drenched with blood.

Gage's last man standing had fended off the twelve-gauge and now aimed his revolver squarely at the marshal. Even as his finger tightened on the trigger, he just couldn't resist a little bluster.

'You've had your six, you son of a bitch!'

Dropping his Remington like a hot coal, Rance desperately attempted to swing his rifle into line, but in his heart he knew he just wouldn't make it.

CHAPTER THIRTEEN

The gunshot came from a completely unexpected quarter and Rance jerked with surprise at the simultaneous blast of pressure next to his head. His would be killer staggered back under the hammer blow to his chest. As the luckless gun thug coughed blood, his trigger finger finally contracted, but the bullet merely erupted towards an empty sky.

With apparently nobody left to fight, Rance twisted around in search of his saviour. His eyes settled on Angie's shapely figure and he shook his head with a mixture of amazement and relief.

'Accept it, Toller,' she demanded with mock formality. 'You just can't get by without me!'

Under any other circumstances he would have burst out laughing, but with Holliday wounded and dead bodies everywhere, the best he could manage was a grateful smile. After scanning the otherwise deserted street for possible threats, he moved anxiously over to his friend's side. Holliday's thigh was leaking blood, but it appeared to be just a flesh wound: a fact that produced an unusual reaction.

'Thought I'd got the job done, this time,' he wearily announced. 'Don't pay me no mind, Rance. This'll keep. Go latch onto Gage, before that cockchafer stirs up any more trouble. And take Angie with you. She's probably got more sense than the two of us put together.'

Accepting Holliday's inescapable logic, Rance joined his intrepid lover and side by side, the two of them cautiously approached Hafford's Saloon. After moving through the battered entrance, they paused for a moment to allow their eyes to adjust to the dim light. A heavily sweating barkeeper stood behind his counter as though rooted to the spot, whilst at the far end of the room two men waited expectantly.

E.B. Gage's jaw dropped in his blistered and bloodied face as he scrutinized the two arrivals. He hadn't seen either of them before, but their identity was obvious. Obvious and quite remarkable. Off to his right, there was a sharp intake of breath from County Sheriff Johnny Behan.

'Holy shit,' that man murmured quietly.

Rance swung the muzzle of his Winchester over to cover the bartender. 'Get out from behind there and over to the end of the room where I can see you. And keep your hands in sight.' As the nervous individual complied, he added, 'Is that Gage down there?'

The man nodded silently as he scurried off to stand near the mining boss. Surprisingly, Gage stayed where he was and it was Behan who advanced to intercept Rance. Keeping his hands clear of any weapons, he nevertheless announced, 'I'm going to have to place you under arrest, Toller. You've destroyed half the town!'

Rance kept moving until there was just a rifle's length between them. His steely eyes settled on those of his fellow lawman. 'I don't reckon anybody is going to arrest me today, Behan. Besides, it's still *my* town. You don't have any jurisdiction here.' With that, he brushed past the startled sheriff and continued on towards the fleshy businessman.

As Behan was about to remonstrate with him, he suddenly realized that Angie had remained in position. Her cocked revolver was pointing directly at the sheriff's midriff and she displayed every intention of using it.

'I've already killed two men today. So do you still intend putting me on the Contention Stage?' she demanded with real menace. 'Or has that idea gone right out of your head?'

Sheriff Behan paled visibly and unintentionally took a step back.

Angie favoured him with a frosty smile. 'That's what I figured. Now you just stay here with me while Rance takes care of business.'

Rance had come to a halt in front of E.B. Gage. That man had reluctantly struggled to his feet and was attempting to present a severe demeanour.

'You Gage?' Rance demanded with studied insolence.

The other man did his best to maintain some dignity. 'It's *Mr* Gage to you!'

The lawman had a novel way of responding to such bluster. With brutal force, he swung the stock of his Winchester into *Mr* Gage's midriff. Accompanied by a massive expulsion of breath, the overweight businessman groaned with pain and involuntarily dropped to his knees. As his eyes began to water, he suddenly realized that he was all alone. All his hired thugs were either dead or gone and no amount of money and influence could extricate him from this fix.

Rance was building up a head of steam that was likely to have only one lethal conclusion. 'You arrogant pig,' he snarled and abruptly jabbed the rifle muzzle into Gage's forehead. '*Nobody* runs me out of my own town!'

The other man snapped his eyes shut and wailed out, 'For pity's sake, mister, don't shoot me. I'll do anything you want.'

Tears of pain rapidly became tears of self-pity, but Rance was unmoved. The *peace officer* was in a vicious frame of mind and had a hankering to kill again. It helped that the snivelling wretch before him was sufficiently pathetic as to deserve it.

E.B. Gage's salvation came from an unlikely quarter. Mayor John Clum never could keep his distance from something newsworthy. For sure, he had no liking for the condescending mining boss, but the man's violent death would undoubtedly only harm Tombstone's prospects. Cautiously edging nearer, he began to talk in a soothing tone.

'Don't go making this into something bad, Rance. Like as not those others deserved to die, but this tub of lard surely doesn't. And besides, he isn't worth the trouble you'll attract. If you kill him, the mine's investors'll have you hunted down like a dog. He's too important for this town's future.'

For what seemed like an age, the marshal remained with his forefinger clenched around the trigger. Then, very slowly, the tension seemed to ease out of his body. Gage's terrified features remained before Rance's rifle, but the compulsive urge to kill had left him. Yet if the mining boss thought that his troubles were over, he was sadly mistaken.

His oppressor withdrew the Winchester a few inches and then rammed it forward … hard. With a wail of anguish at the pain exploding through his forehead, Gage rocked back and finally lost any semblance of self-control. Collapsing to the bar room floor, he began to weep unrestrainedly.

Rance regarded him with distaste. 'I reckon the mayor's right. You ain't worth a bullet. But I'll tell you this. If anything else happens to me and mine while we're in Tombstone, I'll finish the job. So help me God. Savvy?'

With that, he began to repeatedly kick Gage's right leg until the quivering businessman cried out, 'Yes. Yes. I believe you. For Christ's sake, just leave me be!'

The marshal grunted and turned away in disgust. Regarding the mayor dubiously, he remarked, 'It's all your fault I got into this mess.' Then, patting his jacket, he added, 'If you try to hold on to my wages, I'll put this last stick of dynamite where the sun don't shine.'

John Clum gulped nervously, before extending his hands in submission. 'I never knew they'd take against you so. I genuinely wanted law in Tombstone.'

Rance's mood had moderated and he chuckled softly. 'Bet you've had a belly full of it now though, huh?' Before Clum could answer, he added, 'I've got some prisoners to collect from outside of town. How's about you find a new hotel for Doc and Angie? The last one wasn't very satisfactory.'

Back in the street, Rance found his two companions awaiting him expectantly.

'Didn't hear no gunshots,' remarked Holliday dryly. 'What did you do, slit his throat?'

'There'll be no more killing,' the marshal replied. 'Clum's going to organize us some rooms in the Cosmopolitan Hotel. And you need that wound seen to. Meantime, I'm going to fetch Ringo and his crew and put them behind bars. And if that son of a bitch offers me any trouble, he'll find out just what it's like in an unfriendly jail!'

He gazed around at the dead enforcers and his eyes settled on Cullen's blood-soaked body. 'He was pretty good, wasn't he?' he reflected moodily. 'It's a pure shame all this had to happen.'

After affectionately stroking Angie on her cheek, he turned away to find his horse. Behind him, Holliday's hacking cough started up again, only this time it went on and on....

The sun had barely moved across the sky before Marshal Toller returned. His deadpan expression convincingly masked an inner turmoil, but the object that accompanied him would have shocked anyone possessing a shred of sensitivity. The lawman led a single horse and draped across it was Drew Williams's dreadfully bludgeoned, lifeless body.

In his brief absence, Tombstone had sprung back to life. It seemed as though every resident had spilled out onto the streets to view the destruction. Mercy gunshots sounded over at the Pioneer Corral as the injured animals were put down. The undertaker was already measuring his clients for their coffins, but paused long enough to accept Rance's gruesome offering. As that man moved on, expressions varied from curiosity to hostility, but no one displayed any kind of 'trigger itch'. They knew only too well what *their* marshal was capable of.

'It appears my business here has concluded,' he informed Mayor Clum in the lobby of the Cosmopolitan. 'Ringo's high-tailed it and the town doesn't want my brand of law anymore. It's just a damn pity that Wells Fargo man had to take such a beating.'

Clum nodded solemnly. In truth, he felt a large measure

of guilt at the way in which the lawman had been treated. 'So what will you do now?' he queried hesitantly. 'Have you and Angie anywhere to go?'

For the first time since arriving in Tombstone, doubt registered on Rance's strong features. Uncertainty was one thing he found hard to handle. 'You know, I honestly couldn't say. I didn't figure on being out of a job this quick.' He offered a wry smile. 'I guess I'll just have to put it to the brains of the partnership.'

As it turned out, Angie didn't get the chance to offer an opinion. Unbeknown to either of them, both hers and Rance's future had been mapped out since they accepted Doc Holliday's friendship. The 'sporting man' lay on the large double bed in a sumptuous room untouched by either bullets or dynamite.

'I'm dying, Rance,' he croaked. 'Not just some day, but real soon. Thought it best to keep it from you until now.'

The newly unemployed lawman was taken aback. 'Nonsense. That's just a flesh wound. It won't even slow you down.'

Holliday shook his head impatiently. 'I'm talking about my lungs. They're shot. And when I go, it's not gonna be in some town like this, with a load of vultures waiting around for me to die, so's they can take pictures and haggle over my belongings!'

Angie sat on the bed next to him and gently patted his shoulder. She could see spots of fresh blood clinging to his luxuriant moustache and great sadness came over her. 'If you were to stop smoking and drinking, your condition might ease,' she suggested hopefully.

He smiled ruefully up at her. 'A man's got to have a little pleasure. I've been smoking since I was twelve, so I'm not going to stop now and whiskey tastes a mite better than water. Anyhow, the thing is, I've heard of a place called Colorado Springs.' He winked at her. 'That's in Colorado, you know. Apparently the air is dry and fresh and there's places called sanatoriums to help people like me.'

Characteristically, Rance got straight to the point. 'What are you working up to, Doc?'

Holliday conveniently coughed more blood into his handkerchief before answering. 'I want you and Angie to go with me to Colorado. I don't want to die alone and there's no one else I can ask. Wyatt would have helped me, but he's ... elsewhere at the moment.' He paused to gauge their reaction, before adding slyly, 'Personally I think you'd both enjoy the mountain air. And a break from killing folks will do you good. So what do you say? Are you with me?'

Rance stared fixedly at him for long moments, before glancing over at Angie. In turn she watched him expectantly, waiting to see if he made the right decision. Everything suddenly became very clear to Rance. Out of the blue, he had a new purpose in life and that suited him just fine.

'Well, I guess we'll just have to bite the bullet,' he replied with mock reluctance. Then, more positively he asked, 'So when do we leave?' and was rewarded with a beaming smile of approval from his lover. She might have been a little less enamoured of him, had she known that his reasons were not entirely selfless.

As it turned out, they had another reason to leave. Two days after their discussion, John Clum visited Rance and Angie's bedroom. He was noticeably wary of her, but his words seemed genuine enough. 'Gage is still smarting over what you've done and he's getting a bit of his old sass back. He's wired the territorial capital for a Deputy U.S. Marshal. He wants you arrested for something … anything and he's got the political clout.'

Rance shook his head. 'I should have shot that pus weasel when I had the chance. How long before a marshal gets here?'

'There's a railroad link from Prescott to Tucson, so he *could* be here in a couple of days.'

'God damn it,' Rance protested. 'And here's me just getting used to the lap of luxury.' He glanced over at Angie. 'Are you up to travelling again?'

She looked around at the comfortable furnishings, before nodding ruefully. 'Yeah, my shoulder is healing up well.'

Mind made up, Rance announced, 'Right then, we leave tomorrow. It's just a crying shame I never caught up with Ringo. He deserved to hang for what he did to Williams.'

So it was that early the next morning, the three travellers left the Dexter Feed and Livery Stables and rode down 4th Street heading south. They had told no one of their destination, but they weren't taking any chances. Only when they were a few miles beyond the town limits and out of sight of all the rooftops did they swing round and follow their true course: *northeast.*

'You'd think someone would have had the courtesy to see us off, after all we've done for the town,' remarked Holliday sarcastically.

'Oh, I'm pretty sure somebody did,' Rance retorted. 'And

at least we got paid in full. That mayor was a little reluctant to fork out your deputy's wages at first, but he came around to my way of thinking.'

Angie laughed. 'It's funny how people usually do.'

As the three of them companionably rode almost knee-to-knee, Rance put one question that he really should have asked sooner. 'Just how far is it to this Colorado Springs, anyhow?'

Holliday regarded him with a fairly convincing display of embarrassment. 'Well … by going diagonally across New Mexico, I'd say it's roughly about 600 miles.'

Rance's eyes widened incredulously. 'And all of it Apache country, I suppose?'

'Some,' the other man allowed, before favouring Angie with what he hoped was a reassuring smile. 'But you needn't worry yourself, my dear. We're well armed and well mounted. They're mostly on the lookout for slow moving freight wagons and the like, on recognized trails that they can set an ambush for. Stuff they can steal. Food and ammunition.'

'That eases my mind plenty, Doc,' she remarked dryly. 'It looks like this journey is going to be a walk in the park.'

For the next few days, the trio angled towards the New Mexican border. Angie's shoulder was sufficiently recovered for her to be able to discard the sling, but a long journey in such harsh terrain was never going to be easy. As Rance regarded her weary, travel stained figure, he felt troubled.

'This wasn't really what I meant when I promised you a better life,' he announced earnestly, as the two of them rode on ahead of Holliday for a while. 'If I hadn't stopped that stage hold-up, none of this would have happened.'

She was quick to scotch his concern. 'You didn't do that. *We* did. And but for that, you might have ended up digging in the ground like some gopher and we would have never met Doc. What we're doing now is the right thing.'

As far as she was concerned that was an end to it. Rance could not help but admire her for it. And he knew damn well that he wasn't cut out to be any kind of silver prospector either.

Holliday's wound showed no sign of infection, which was a relief, because he had plenty more things to worry about. His breathing became worse, with sustained coughing fits that were gradually and irrevocably weakening him. It was only his iron determination to reach his hoped for sanctuary that kept him going.

Their supplies were supplemented by food stops at ranches and small settlements along the way. They politely refused all offers of accommodation and avoided towns, because Rance was wary of word of their presence getting back to the federal authorities. It was at the last of these stops that he was served with tainted meat, masked by chillies.

'For two bits, I'd go back there and feed him the barrel of this Remington,' Rance swore later, but both of his companions doubted that. For some time he had barely been able to sit his saddle properly and had to keep disappearing into the scrub to relieve himself. It was because of this that they made camp early that night. Although it was mostly open country, they stumbled upon an arroyo that hid them from prying eyes and gave them the confidence to build a small fire, mainly at Holliday's insistence.

'I just can't cope without some hot coffee,' he proclaimed. 'It's the only thing keeping me going.'

'Sweet Jesus. I wish I could *stop* going,' Rance rejoined. Although still looking pale and washed out, in truth he seemed to be on the mend. 'I think I'll try me a plate of those beans, Angie. I feel real sharp set.'

'You sure?' she queried doubtfully, but spooned some out for him anyway.

As they ate, the sun eased down below the horizon and darkness fell fast.

Rance glanced around uneasily. 'Once that coffee's gone, we should douse the fire. Even down here it's like a god damn beacon.' He peered at the others in search of agreement and then let out a groan. His guts had contracted like a vice and he abruptly knew what he needed to do ... fast. Instinctively grabbing his rifle, he groaned again and heaved himself to his feet. Almost doubled over, he staggered off into the darkness until he was completely out of sight of his companions.

'Let's hope he doesn't shit on a centipede in the dark,' Holliday remarked drolly. 'Those critters are worse than any rattlers.' Then, almost inevitably, he began to cough. It was this noise that drowned out the stealthy approach of creatures just as dangerous as any centipede.

CHAPTER FOURTEEN

'Hello, the fire,' hailed a disturbingly close male voice. It was immediately followed by the distinctive sound of a revolver being cocked. 'Thought we might sample some of your coffee. That's if you folks run a friendly camp.'

Holliday stifled his coughing and reached for the sawn-off, which by tacit agreement he had retained following the bloodshed in Tombstone. Eyes wide with fear, Angie grabbed for her revolver. Unfortunately, the presence of firelight worked against them. From two other locations around them came the menacing sound of other weapons being readied.

'Now that really ain't very sociable,' continued the disembodied voice. 'But if you want to play it that way, think on this. You're highlighted by that cosy little fire and there's three repeaters aimed at you right now.'

Angie and Holliday stared at each other and after a moment he emphatically shook his head. Then, very reluctantly, he placed the shotgun on the ground and Angie followed suit.

'Very sensible,' came the triumphant reply and footsteps sounded around the camp. Three men, two of them wearing red sashes and all looking the worse for wear, converged on them. Holliday inhaled sharply as he recognized the leader. Firelight flickered on Johnny Ringo's lean, brutalized features and he chuckled gleefully.

'Well, well. This *is* a turn up. The marshal's bitch and a lying, thieving cardsharp. What do you say, lunger? Still reckon you could take me?'

Holliday regarded him distastefully. 'On my worst day, I know I could.'

Ringo sniggered. 'Well, I'll tell you. You don't look so good to me. I reckon we'll have to go at it.'

'Just watch him, Johnny,' one of his cronies muttered. 'I've seen him do some things.'

'Shut up, Ed,' Ringo barked, before turning his attention to Angie. Suspicion now registered on his features. 'So where are your horses and where's that god damned law dog?'

Angie was level-headed enough to recognize that this was the critical moment. If she got it wrong now, then they were all dead. The fact that their *three* horses were hobbled to allow the animals to forage in the sparse landscape meant that they had not been discovered ... yet. Even as she made up her mind, she could sense Holliday's eyes boring into her.

In a strident voice, the frightened young woman launched into a bitter tirade. 'As far as I'm concerned, Rance Toller can burn in hell. He's not worth a plug nickel. He took up with some painted whore in the Occidental and I don't play second fiddle to no one!'

As she had hoped, that got Johnny Ringo's full attention. He intently looked her up and down as she squatted in front of the fire. That he liked what he saw was obvious.

'In a way that's a shame. We'd hoped to settle some

scores with him, hadn't we, boys?' Completely ignoring the enthusiastic gestures of his cronies, he continued with, 'It's no thanks to him that we all survived that blood fest down at Clanton's place. And as you can see, we're all armed to the teeth again. We met up with some freighters who had more than they needed, ha ha.'

The outlaw fell silent for a few moments as his eyes lingered on her body. It was obvious that Rance Toller was no longer uppermost on his mind. 'How could a feisty little gal like you go off with this lunger?' he queried incredulously. 'I'd treat you better than he ever could.'

It was her turn to display shocked surprise. 'The last time you saw me, you shot me,' she accused hotly, wondering all the time just where the hell Rance had got to.

Ringo grinned lasciviously at her. 'Why hold that against me? You're still alive, aren't you?'

It was at that very moment that the third rustler made a discovery. 'Sweet Jesus, Johnny. There's *three* horses out there!'

The ghastly reality of that announcement registered in Ringo's head and he twisted around in alarm. From the impenetrable gloom behind Angie, there came a muzzle flash and the loud report of a powerful rifle. The man known as Ed 'shut up' for good, as a bullet from Rance's Winchester removed the top of his head in an explosion of gore.

Reacting with practised speed, Ringo loosed off three rapid shots in the direction of the flash and then shifted position to get clear of the firelight. Even as he did so, two things occurred that tipped the balance of the shootout. Rance had obviously adhered to the 'fire and move' rule, because another bullet exploded out of the darkness and slammed into Ringo's other sidekick, sending him staggering back. Tripping over his own boots, the unfortunate man, still suffering from the wound received at the Clanton Ranch, tumbled into the fire. He lay there, helpless and twitching as his life ebbed away.

Simultaneously, the two hammers on Holliday's shotgun clicked ominously back and Ringo found himself yet again at the wrong end of the 'two-shoot' gun. 'I've got this cur covered, Rance,' the consumptive yelled out. 'Don't you go shooting him now, you hear?' Then more softly he added, 'I want you all to myself, Johnny. It's time we answered the question.'

The sound of a Winchester's lever action operating was audible, but no more shots crashed out. 'I hear you,' came the reply and then a few moments later Rance appeared in the circle of light. He was still clutching his guts, but a broad smile covered his features.

'It's getting so you can't even take a shit in peace out here,' he remarked, before gazing pointedly at the sole remaining outlaw. All traces of humour left him as he added, 'I was hoping to catch up with you again.'

Ringo sneered at him, before turning his malignant attention to Angie. 'Very clever, little lady. I won't forget this. You suckered me good.'

'I know and I'm glad,' she retorted.

With their noses yet again twitching under the assault of the sickly sweet smell of burning flesh, Rance snapped out a command. 'Drag your friend out of that fire, before we all choke to death.'

Although very conscious of the deadly twelve gauge covering his every move, Ringo nonetheless casually holstered his Colt, rather than discarding it and then heaved the charred corpse to one side. 'He was no friend of mine,' he remarked dismissively. 'Besides, he looks a sight underdone for my tastes.' Then he turned to face Rance and arrogantly demanded, 'Now what? You going to arrest me again? Because somehow I don't see you hauling me all the way back to Tombstone to stand trial. And yet, paroling me to Jesus in cold blood just ain't your style.'

'You don't deserve to live after what you did to Mr Williams,' Angie cut in angrily.

It was Doc Holliday who offered the solution that he had already touched on. 'The only reason he's still packing that six-gun is because he's going to get the chance to use it.'

Ringo's dark features clouded as he heard the implication. 'I've got no beef with you, lunger. It's this poxy lawman that's been dogging my footsteps.'

'Nevertheless it's me you're going to face, boy,' Holliday persisted coldly. 'It's said by some misguided folks that you're the deadliest pistolero in the southwest. So now we're going to find out.'

'You right sure about this, Doc?' Rance queried unhappily. 'We could always just hang him as a common rustler.'

Holliday smiled. 'You see any trees around here? Besides, it'll be interesting. I figure I've got less to lose than him.' With that, he carefully handed the scatter-gun over to Angie and then moved off a few paces, so that he and Ringo faced each other across the fire.

'You've likely got three chambers left in that Colt. That should be enough to finish me, *if* you get lucky.'

Johnny Ringo suddenly didn't like the odds. A sheen of sweat coated his forehead as he glanced at the two spectators.

'What the hell kind of deal is this? If I kill you, they'll get me anyway.'

'It's about as good as you gave Drew Williams,' Rance responded harshly. 'And you don't think I've forgotten about Angie either, do you? When I interrupted you robbing the Tucson Stage, you said that you were born to die. So just get to it!'

The outlaw pondered for a moment and then shrugged fatalistically. With his chosen lifestyle, it oftentimes just didn't pay to worry overmuch about consequences. Dismissing Rance and Angie from his mind, he concentrated solely on the hunched figure of Doc Holliday. That man stifled a cough and allowed his right hand to hover near his gun butt. Ringo did likewise and together they began to slowly circle the campfire, like swordsmen searching for an opening.

Flickering shadows played on their drawn features. Ringo licked suddenly dry lips.

He was looking for some kind of edge. Anything that might distract his opponent. Then Holliday lazily winked his left eye and it happened. Both men drew simultaneously. They moved so fast that to the two onlookers it all seemed like a blur. Two shots rang out, except that one ever so slightly preceded the other. As a swirl of dust kicked up next to Holliday's boots, Ringo's eyes widened in shock and disbelief at the bullet that had ploughed into his skull directly between them. As the *so-called* deadliest pistolero in the southwest died on his feet, his killer theatrically twirled his smoking revolver and then slotted it neatly back into its holster.

'You came close, mister,' he announced smugly. 'But no cigar!'

Rance and Angie gazed at him in wonder for long moments. Even though sudden death no longer held any surprises for them, both knew that they had just witnessed something special. It was the man that finally broke the silence. Smiling fondly at his lover he remarked, 'And don't even suggest burying those fellas. They don't deserve it and I ain't wasting my sweat on them.'

Fittingly, it was Doc Holliday who had the last word. 'You realize that if I'd lost, it would have saved you one hell of a long journey.'